'Don't come near me now.'

Ana halted. 'Why not?'

'Because I want to kiss you. I want to do more than kiss you.'

Thwack. The ball hit the tree again. And her legs could hardly hold her up.

'You have no idea what I want to do to you,' Seb muttered, fists clenched, muscles bulging. His bare torso shone with sweat. He was primed.

Heat flooded in her most secret places. And she was the one panting, as if she was the one doing the crazy workout in the heat of the afternoon.

He stopped, stood with his hands on his hips and glared at her. 'We started something back then, Ana. And for me it isn't over. I thought it was. But it isn't.'

TO LOVE, HONOUR AND DISOBEY

BY
NATALIE ANDERSON

First published in Great Britain 2010
Harlequin Mills & Boon Limited,
Eton House, 18-24 Paradise Road, Richmond, Surrey TW9 1SR

© Natalie Anderson 2010

ISBN: 978 0 263 87731 1

Harlequin Mills & Boon policy is to use papers that are natural, renewable and recyclable products and made from wood grown in sustainable forests. The logging and manufacturing process conform to the legal environmental regulations of the country of origin.

Printed and bound in Spain
by Litografia Rosés, S.A., Barcelona

Possibly the only librarian who got told off herself for talking too much, **Natalie Anderson** decided writing books might be more fun than shelving them—and, boy, is it that! Especially writing romance—it's the realisation of a lifetime dream kick-started by many an afternoon spent devouring Grandma's Mills & Boon® novels… She lives in New Zealand, with her husband and four gorgeous-but-exhausting children. Swing by her website any time—she'd love to hear from you: www.natalie-anderson.com

Recent titles by the same author:

HOT BOSS, BOARDROOM MISTRESS
BETWEEN THE ITALIAN'S SHEETS
PLEASURED IN THE PLAYBOY'S PENTHOUSE
BOUGHT: ONE NIGHT, ONE MARRIAGE

CHAPTER ONE

ANA didn't know what she was going to do with all the photos. She'd taken hundreds—and hadn't the heart to delete a single one of them. Good thing she'd brought an extra couple of flash cards with her. Africa was everything she'd hoped it would be—wide, wild and incredibly hot. Totally different from anything she'd experienced and she sought to capture it—so she could hold onto the sense of freedom when she returned home.

Even now, with the truck pulled over to the side of the road on the outskirts of Arusha, she had her camera up and ready. She leaned her head over the side to see what it was that Bundy, the driver, was doing. Talking to someone. She could see him smiling up at the stranger who had his back to her.

Ana smiled too, enjoying the view. Bundy's friend was quite a specimen of a male. Ana let the sensation wash over her—for the first time in almost a year having a pleasurable physical reaction to a man. A sliver of excitement sparked in her belly, the momentary wondering— *what if*? She wriggled in her seat and angled her head for a better look. Oh, yeah. A definite what if.

She giggled. Fantastic, finally she was back to normal. Whole, healthy and actually able to feel a touch of sexual heat. She lifted the camera, clicked a couple of times. And then zoomed.

Denim shorts showed off strong, bronze calves and hinted that the thighs were equally muscular. Hands rested on narrow hips accentuating a great butt. But it was the shoulders that got her. His torso was one hell of a wide triangle—so wide the fabric of his shirt pulled slightly at the seams. Broad, broad shoulders that were built to be hung onto. The kind of physique to make a woman feel ultra feminine—and as Ana was such a giantess she needed a big man to make her feel feminine. Unfortunately there weren't enough of them around, and when she did find the occasional one he was never interested in her. For some reason big men always seemed to want petite women. But she could forget that reality for now and just enjoy this present fantasy. She took another picture. His hair was cropped close—almost army kind of close. The tips of her fingers tingled, wondering what it would be like to run her hands over his scalp. *Interesting*.

But the best thing definitely was his height. Bundy wasn't short but this guy was a good half head taller than him. Being so horrendously tall herself, Ana had always been drawn to very tall men and he had height in abundance. In fact this guy—from the back at least—had everything. Now if only he'd turn around and fulfil the whole fantasy of male-model gorgeousness.

She shifted her grip on the camera, wriggling her fingers to let out the tension sparking in her muscles. Sex. She was actually thinking about sex.

Wow.

She half laughed again and took another picture. Knowing it was stupid but loving the freedom to enjoy a beautiful male. She hadn't thought she'd ever have it in her again. After the hell of the last year it was great to discover she did. All she had to do now was return to London and hopefully find the paperwork complete. At last she could get on with everything. She'd known coming here was the right thing to do. And now she'd had the final proof of her recovery and the return of her zest for life—and her libido.

Bundy turned and the two men walked away from her around the front of the truck where she could no longer see them. No matter, she looked at the screen on her camera, smiled her way through the few snaps of the handsomest back view of a boy she'd ever seen.

Ever.

She smiled again. She was over it. She was finally, totally over it.

There was a bang and a bump and the truck jolted forward—on the move again. She glanced up as the others called out. It took a moment for her to realise there was someone new on board and that her fellow passengers were saying hi to him. That he was slowly walking down the aisle towards her. His gaze direct, relentless and inscrutable.

Ana hadn't known it was possible to be frozen by flaming heat. She couldn't move, couldn't think and couldn't believe her eyes. Yet somehow she was breathing, somehow she was seeing and sadly there was no denying *who* she was seeing. And she had to believe it.

'Seb?' Did she even say it aloud?

He was the one wearing denims cut off at the knee and the casual tee that totally showed off his broad shoulders. *He* was the one with his hair cropped sexy soldier short. *He* was the one standing so tall and making Bundy laugh.

He was the one inspiring her frisky fantasy—the first she'd had in *months*.

Oh, my, it was too ironic.

She blinked, hoping like hell she was seeing things. But no. It really was Sebastian.

Her brain sent instant freeze messages to the melting softness in her body. She had just been eyeing up her ex.

Sebastian Rentoul. Her one and only one-night stand. Her one and only week-long fling. Her one and only whirlwind wedding.

Her husband. The father of her baby.

Her husband who had lied. Her baby who had died.

A thousand images flashed in the space of a second. The heat and light in the bar, the thrum of the beat as they'd stood so close, the lust in the touch, the laughter as they'd come together and uttered those foolish words. The anger in discovery of betrayal and mis-communication. The anguish in her lonely loss.

She hadn't been granted the joy of knowing her child. Looking back on it, she hadn't known her husband either. The man she'd fallen for was a fiction—a fantasy in her own needy head and heart.

It was excruciating what a fool she'd been. And the resulting pain had almost broken her completely.

Suck it up, Ana. Suck it up.

It was done. In the past and she was over it. She wasn't going to fall apart at the mere sight of him. For one thing he didn't know the half of it. And she didn't want him to. She blinked again. He was coming towards her. She reeled it all in—stuffing the memories, and emotion, into her internal prison and padlocking the door. She shut off the camera and set it on her lap, not wanting him to see the pictures she'd just been giggling over. Good grief. That she'd just felt the burn for him?

She looked down. Moved faster when she saw it, twisting the thick platinum band off her finger. He definitely didn't need to see she still wore his wedding ring. She hadn't taken it off in all these months. She'd been going to. Of course she had. But she'd been told wearing one was something a lone woman traveller could do to try to deflect unwanted interest—and as she'd had it already…

She tucked it into her camera case. Even so, her tan exposed a pale ring of skin on her finger. But she could do nothing about it now. He wouldn't notice— he wouldn't be getting that close. She darted another look.

He was almost right beside her. Had a smile on but it wasn't full strength. Not the knockout 'come party with me' number he'd hit her with that first night. Even so it was enough to shoot her temperature up. Too unfair that a guy like him should be given such a gift.

She summoned a bright smile of her own, ignoring her scattered insides. Pride dictated she keep it together.

'Wow. Sebastian.' OK so she sounded a little breathless. No surprise given the way her thoughts and her blood raced.

Unbelievable. Here he was looking totally at home as if he were the one who'd been on safari in Africa for the best part of the month. He even had a tan—she knew it took only moments in the sun for his skin to go that gorgeous burnished brown. It had done that during those few crazy days in Gibraltar. Oh, hell, she didn't need to think of that again. From every angle heat crawled over her body, zeroing in on her middle.

'Ana.' He didn't sound breathless. But he did sound quiet. He nodded at the empty seat next to her. 'Mind if I sit here?'

Her smile became that little bit fixed. 'Not at all. Please.' She shifted on her own, moving that imperceptible half-inch nearer the side of the truck and away from him. Her heart thudded harder, all senses on acute alert as she clamped on the muscles.

No way, no way, no way. He couldn't be here. And she couldn't be thinking about…what she'd been thinking about. Not about him. 'Fancy seeing you here,' she said. 'Africa. Of all places.'

He sat and the devilishness showed in his grin. 'Quite some coincidence, isn't it?'

'Quite.' As if it really were. 'Who told you I was here?'

'No one,' he said innocently. 'It really is a coincidence.'

Yeah, right.

He turned, watching her too close, sitting too close. 'Oh, I got the divorce papers.'

Oh, so he was just going to throw that in casually, huh? Ana made her smile even sweeter. 'Did you sign them?'

Please, please, please. Then this really would be over.

'Not yet.'

Her heart skidded.

'I wanted to see you first.'

'Oh.' *Why?* Hadn't everything been said and done? Or rather not said and not done, which was frankly the way she'd prefer to keep it. They totally didn't need a post-mortem. It had been a stupid, mad mistake and the best thing to do now was wipe the slate clean and move on. *Away* from each other and as fast as possible given how her body was reacting in such an off-base kind of way.

Sebastian took a couple of big breaths and tried to clear the mess from his head. Hell. He hadn't imagined her being like this. He hadn't imagined her looking like this. All these months when he'd thought of her she'd been quite different—pale, a little shy, compliant.

Here she was tanned, her hair was longer, loose and she was wearing only a singlet top and shorts. She looked light and bright and confident.

OK, so she'd been shocked to see him. The moment of recognition had written it all over her face. Not a pleasant surprise. But she was smiling again now. Eyes veiled for sure. But still a smile—an incredible smile, actually.

'I wanted to see you. I wanted to…' He hesitated. It had ended badly. Less than a week after the wedding there'd been a hell of a row and she'd walked. It had been his fault. And at the time he'd been a bit relieved—sanity had started to return. But then he'd started to wonder. 'I wanted to make sure you're OK.'

It had been a relief to finally hear from her—but just getting the divorce papers wasn't enough. He couldn't just sign them and forget. He had to see her for himself. To be sure. There weren't many things in his life he regretted. But he regretted that week more than anything.

'Well—' her smile didn't falter '—as you can see, I'm fine, Sebastian.'

That hint of challenge in her voice slipped into his blood like a needle shot of deadly virus. His body reacted on the spot. Could it fight it—finally build some defence—or would it succumb to the disease—again?

'Yeah.' He nodded, despite himself. 'You are.'

She was more than fine. The ripple in his body told him that, the rise of temperature, of awareness. He might be looking at her face, but every cell absorbed her slender curves and incredibly long limbs that were so on show in those short, short shorts.

Memories stirred. Memories he'd buried. The scent, the laughter, the sparkle in her eyes and the satin of her skin. And her heat.

He was stifling hot now—it was Africa though, wasn't it?—not because of her. It was the dry, inescapable heat of a continent almost always in drought.

Well, not quite. Because not only was he hot. He was hard. He suppressed the unexpected flare of desire. Surely not. Not going there again. He looked back on that week and it was like this blurred rush of events that had knocked the breath from his lungs and the sense from his head. Even now he couldn't work out how it had happened. How he'd come to commit such folly.

Then he refocused on her. Felt the tightening deep within. And knew. Sexual drive, physical compatibility, instant lust. Whatever you wanted to call it, they'd had it—by the oversized shipping-container load. But they hadn't had anything else. They hadn't had time for anything else—and no interest either. He never had interest in more.

He felt a vague stirring of panic. So he'd seen her. She was fine—clearly absolutely, completely, utterly fine. But now he was stuck on a truck with her for another week. Not well planned, Seb. He wanted to call out to the driver, to get off again, but they were out of the town now and heading towards some national park wilderness. OK. He sat a little further away from her. He could handle this, couldn't he? He could control his more insane animal urges. Hadn't he spent the last year discovering the meaning of discipline?

Ana looked out of the side of the truck and blinked. Trying to stop the fog from clouding her head. She'd forgotten. She'd totally forgotten. OK, so she'd made herself forget. It had been the only way to get through the heartache, by blanking out the electricity that had arced between them. But here it was back again. Like a flash, before she'd even realised it was him—making her body want to bend towards him.

As he was almost six foot five people couldn't help but notice Sebastian—and that was just the height thing. While she knew all about that, that was where their commonality ended. When you added the rest of Seb's body, the smile and the ice-blue eyes, you had an awesome package—something that definitely couldn't be said for her. She was just overly tall, overly angular, overly shy. And there was something more about Seb. Something that transcended the physical. Something that made not just women sit up, but men too. That unspoken authority, his confidence.

A man in control—*the* man in control.

That was Seb. The one everyone said yes to. But she wasn't going to let him take control of them again as he had that week. There *was* no them.

Confidence rippled through her. Yes. She was no longer the pushover he'd met back then. In fact the strength she now had was partly a result of his attention. There might have been nothing else, but that extreme passion had been something for her to cling to. No one had ever wanted her—or indeed had her— the way Sebastian had in that week. And for someone to have wanted her like that—even for just a short time—had been a huge boost to her self-esteem. For the first time in her life she'd felt beautiful. Such a shame, then, wasn't it, that what had then happened had happened? But she'd learned from it—moved on and become determined to make something more of herself. Really she ought to thank him for giving her the fuel, the firepower to finally take charge of her life.

'So you're joining the truck?'

'Yeah.'

Oh, well. That was going to be interesting. 'It's almost over.' No hiding the thank-goodness-for-that in her tone. She smiled brighter to make up for it.

'I'm staying on for a bit after.' He grinned too, as if he knew her sentiments and understood the relief. 'Doing some sightseeing on my own.'

'Great.' Good luck to him. She'd be on the plane and getting on with her life. But before then they had a week to get through. She processed the thought:

they didn't need to mix together much—could sit apart. Yet it was such a small environment on the truck. If only she'd made more of an effort with the other passengers she could hide amongst them. But she'd kept herself to herself—just quietly taking in the sights and enjoying her freedom.

The truck bounced along the road taking them further from the village. For once Bundy seemed intent on picking up the speed. Ana kept her focus on the vast landscape, enjoying the slight wind cooling her burning skin. It was a converted old army truck. The tarpaulin roof was invariably pulled right back so they could see all around, and be slow cooked in the sun. Only it was no slow cooker today—she felt as if she were being grilled on high.

The bang was loud. She lurched forward, bumped her head on the seat in front of her and in the same instant was thrown back into her seat.

'Ow.' It was the shock more than anything that made her cry out.

Swearing voices seemed to surround her. Loud and lots. Bundy in the cab hollered up an apology and an explanation. A blown tyre. She kept her eyes closed, feeling sick at the way her brain still rattled back and forth against her skull.

Fingers gripped her shoulder. Skin touched skin. She was compelled to turn. The sizzle kick-started her heart and she squeezed her eyes tighter together. Not wanting to acknowledge what he made her feel.

'Ana, are you OK?'

She said nothing.

'Ana?' His fingers moved, stroking her shoulder, her arm. Every spot he touched burned. It was a wonder the smoke wasn't curling up between them as he kindled her senses.

She opened her eyes. Looked straight into the face that was so familiar yet was so different. Leaner, somehow more taut. He was looking right back at her—too close; their gaze locked. Instantly the voices of the others were muted. She heard nothing but the growing rush in her ears. It had been so very long. So long since her toes had curled in instinctive delight, so long since she'd felt that restlessness inside.

Her brain was thickening, but her blood thinning— zinging with mercurial fluidity around her body. She was melting, her core defrosting as yearning rose— for the passion that once made her mindless. His passion.

Her lips parted but no sound emerged. Mesmerised, she watched the lights shift in his eyes. The pale blue sharpened—reflected the shock. Then his pupils swelled, the darkness swallowing the ice. She could see the tension as the tiny muscles worked,narrowing his gaze just that little bit.

Her own eyes were fixed wide—she couldn't blink, couldn't breathe.

After an age his attention dropped. She could feel his focus. Could read his mind and for just one moment she wanted it.

A kiss.

She jerked, pulling away from him. Concussion. Had to be. That could be the only explanation for that random moment of *lunacy*.

His hand fell and she heard him mutter the word she'd once ached to hear.

'Sorry.'

So was she. Sorry he'd just walked back into her life. Even sorrier that her body seemed determined to celebrate the fact.

'I'm going to help with the tyre.' He stood.

She pasted another smile on her face as if that half-second had never happened. 'Great.'

A week with Seb on board. She could handle that. Sure she could. No problem.

CHAPTER TWO

ANA spent the next minute reminding herself that although Sebastian Rentoul had made her feel truly desired for the first time in her life, he had also been the cause of her darkest heartache. He'd been the flame that had burned through her until all that had been left inside was cold ash. The loss she'd felt took her breath away—her life's blood. And he had no idea.

The only thing that mattered to him was his job. In that he was ruthless—viciously determined. He did whatever it took to climb to the top—wasn't that why he'd done what he had with her? They'd been a one-night stand that went on a few days too long—a weekend getaway that had culminated in a wedding. Ana had been infatuated; she understood that now. Intoxicated by his desire for her, overwhelmed by how right she had felt in his arms. For once she hadn't been too tall, or awkward. They'd been so physical her usual reticence hadn't mattered—they'd been too busy to talk. She'd breathlessly, brainlessly said yes. And she'd been so excited about their future.

But it had lasted less than a week. Because when they had returned to London, and he to work, she'd found out about his promotion—the one that had depended on him stabilising his personal life. It wasn't that he'd fallen head over heels for her at all. He'd simply needed a wife—and she'd been the malleable fling of the moment. The naïve fool.

When she'd accused him of it he hadn't been shy about admitting it, ruthlessly acknowledging that he had no real belief in marriage—that he'd never meant it to be for ever. And so she'd found out—too late—that his life was one big game. He was a playboy. And he'd played her. Sebastian Rentoul got everything and anything and any*one* he wanted. That conversation had been short and brutal. She'd walked out—run away. But for her, the worst had yet to come.

So in the end it took only thirty seconds to underline why she was definitely, totally, not going there again. But it was half an hour until the tyre was changed and they got back on board. Seb returned to the seat next to her and her pulse was still too fast, too erratic.

There was nothing for her to do but box on through it. 'How's work going?'

He sent her an ironic look. 'It's going well. Lots of cases. I've been working long hours.'

And partying even longer hours, she bet. She'd been wowed when she'd found out he was a lawyer—had been such an ignorant idealist. But Seb wasn't that kind of lawyer. He didn't don wig and gown and go defend the innocent or the persecuted. He did divorce. Representing high-powered wealthy people embroiled in the bitterest of partings.

Seb swung into action for them—dividing, conquering—making sure the cougar kept the house or the serial sleazoid avoided the alimony. Knowing his powers of persuasion, she knew it was a waste of his talent. He should be in the criminal courtroom. He'd have a jury free a man despite evidence caught on camera and with DNA back-up.

'So you got made partner?'

That was why he'd married her. Not because he'd fallen as madly, deeply, passionately for her as she had for him. Not because he too had been swept away by a kind of madness. No, he'd had a far more clay-based reason for proposing than her helium-filled one for saying yes. There'd been some archaic belief in his old-school firm that the partners needed to have a stable, respectable home life. Not the girls-a-go-go playboy lifestyle that Seb had.

She should have figured it out sooner—that he hadn't meant any of it. He'd picked her up in a bar, for heaven's sake—as if that were any real start to a serious relationship? In minutes he'd seduced the brains out of her. Just as he did with a different woman every week. Only she'd been so gullible and needy she'd believed him when he'd said she was special. She'd been stupid enough to step onto a plane with him and take off for a sex-drenched mini-break on an island famed for its sun and sand. An island where, if you were so inclined, you could even get married.

And she'd been so inclined. She'd been so desperate to believe. How badly she'd wanted to believe that someone had fallen in love with her just like that. So stupid—as if that would happen? But a childhood lacking in love and full of loneliness did that to a person.

'Yes.' Seb sighed. 'I checked all the boxes, didn't I? Have wife, will progress.'

'You don't have a wife.'

'I do,' he replied, lifting his hand, showing the wedding band.

'Another one?' She deadpanned, ignoring the spike of adrenalin. 'My God. You're a bigamist.'

He laughed. She stared as his face broke up—she saw his full lips widen, teeth flash and his eyes light. And then there was the sound. It was like having plugs removed from her ears. Hearing that freshness, she felt sweet warmth sweep inside. She couldn't help responding, her lips curving.

'Ana. *We're* married. Still married, in case you'd forgotten.'

Of course she hadn't. She was working to end it, wasn't she? 'We're only married on paper, Seb. And not for much longer.'

'What do you mean only on paper?' His eyes twinkled brighter. 'I remember consummating our marriage, Ana. I remember the night on the balcony. I remember the way you—'

'All right.' She held up her hand, stopping what she knew was going to be a totally inappropriate recollection. 'So I'm your wife. How the hell do you explain it?'

'You don't like city life.' He angled his head and looked at her as if he were a medium reading her mind. 'And for all I know that might actually be true. I decline invitations on your behalf and don't participate in client functions myself. I'm very devoted.'

'To what, my absence?'

'It's very useful.' He nodded. 'I can say no to my lady clients and go up in their esteem at the same time.'

'They really think you have a wife secreted away somewhere?' She was intrigued now. Did he really feed them this rubbish?

'Well, I do, don't I? But they don't know that not even I know where the hell you've been. I have your picture on my desk. Looking soulfully into the lens.'

'You're kidding.' He had to be. 'They honestly believe you?'

'I guess.' Sebastian shrugged. He didn't care what they all thought. Frankly since he'd been so grumpy the questions had stopped early on and he hadn't had to lie—except by omission. And since he'd taken himself right out of the social scene and thrown himself into work, he'd proved himself beyond worthy of the promotion. It was what he should have done in the first place. There'd have been no need for that stupid piece of paper and the confusion that had blown up between them.

He'd laugh about it one day. Honest he would. But until he'd demanded that her best friend Phil finally tell him where the hell she was, he'd always wondered if something had happened to her. Sure she'd left him a message, but when he'd followed up on it he'd discovered it had all been lies. She'd vanished. And he'd been left with that nagging worry. And the regret. He'd been horribly blunt when she'd asked him straight out about why he'd married her. He hadn't meant to hurt her—he'd liked her and had sure as hell liked sleeping with her.

But it only took one look at her now to know that he'd been wrong to worry. She was looking great. So much skin. So much *inviting* skin.

He shouldn't have touched her before. He was here to get closure, not to rekindle that out-of-control flame. 'I think they think you're not well or something,' he said. 'They don't ask any more. Quiet sympathy offered all round.'

'Rather than sex.'

Oh, so she could do sarcasm, could she? He laughed, cringing a little, but he couldn't blame her—after all, he'd told her about the last one, hadn't he? 'They wouldn't dare. Not believing I'm so devoted.'

All those inviting looks had dropped. Had he known it would be so simple he'd have invented a wife a couple of years ago. Saved himself this current mess. Getting made partner at Wilson & Crosbie had been his ambition since before university. He was there now. But there'd been no chance of a partnership while single; the old boys in the firm were ultra-conservative. They didn't want their well-heeled lady clients eyeing him up, or the estranged young wives of their male clients confusing the agenda. And they certainly didn't like the entire secretarial pool coming to a complete halt every time he walked past their desks. And given he'd had a fling with one that had ended with the girl in constant floods of tears at work, maybe they had a point. Apparently they felt he needed a wife.

He'd been going to force it. Point out the ridiculousness to the firm—he was a divorce specialist, for heaven's sake. But that had been just before he'd met Ana. Fate had lent a hand. He'd been so hot for her—whisking her off to have his wicked way. And one afternoon in Gibraltar when he'd been intoxicated by sun and sand and so much glorious sex he'd had the most stupid idea. She'd agreed and they'd married the next day.

Her eyes slid from his. 'So how are you going to explain the divorce?'

He felt the devil surge in him and was unable to stop the temptation to tease. 'Maybe there won't be a divorce.'

'What?' Wide-eyed, she shook her head. 'There'll be one. You can count on it.'

'You're that desperate to be rid of me?' Why? Did she have another man? Where was he? And why was she on a truck cruising around Africa?

'Of course I am.'

'Then why's it taken so long?' It was the best part of a year since she'd walked out and he hadn't heard a word until those papers had landed on his desk.

She looked away, didn't answer directly. 'Don't you want a divorce? Good grief.' Her face flashed back towards him. 'Do you still need a wife to keep your precious job? That's insane.'

He opened his mouth, about to correct her, but she surged on.

'I'll fight you for it, Seb. Don't think I won't. Really you should sign quickly. Otherwise I might go after your money.'

He laughed again, shaking his head at the weakness of her threat. 'No judge would buy it, honey. You're the one who deserted me, remember? After a mere three days of marriage. I'm the wounded party, the heart-broken one. It's more likely that I'd get some of *your* money.' It wasn't, of course, but he'd take the chance of snatching the moral high ground all the same. Just for once.

His smile died. 'Why now, Ana?' Why, after months of silence, of him not knowing where she was, had she sent him the papers now? 'Have you met someone?'

'That's none of your business, Seb.'

It wasn't. But it was the question burning a hole inside him now. Where had she been, what had she been doing this last year? Because she looked good—so mouth-wateringly good. How irritating.

His last year had been nothing but hard work. But until this moment he hadn't put the difficulty directly down to her. He thought it had been the situation that had strangled his usually raging sex drive. That their mess of a marriage and the resulting awkwardness had put him off women for a while. But that 'while' had stretched on and on. He was still totally uninterested in dating. Hadn't even had a casual one-night stand since. Mind you, that was how he'd started with her and he wasn't risking a similar disaster. Besides, he hadn't met anyone who'd pushed his 'on' button.

Except he was switched on now.

By her. He couldn't believe how attracted he still was to her. Well, that was dumb. Because one thing was for sure: it wasn't happening again.

Ana suppressed the sigh and tried really hard not to look at her watch *again*. Every hour seemed to be taking five times as long to pass. Their conversation had just cut out. He'd turned away from her and focused on the scenery. As had she. With rigid determination.

Why hadn't she sent the papers sooner? Because for those first few months she'd been too ill to do anything.

And then when she'd been physically better, emotionally she hadn't been ready to cope. Finally she'd emerged from the darkness—she'd salvaged something from the experience and she'd begun to dream up her business. She'd concentrated on doing a couple of courses—building her confidence, feeling as if she was achieving something. And she'd worked, saved, prepared to relaunch her life. Only then had she been sure she could deal with Seb—or at least instruct her lawyer to.

Finally they arrived at the campsite. It was part of a snake park where they could look at the deadly Black Mamba—apparently it took only one bite and then you had mere moments to write your will. It'd be good if one could get up close to Seb. Or maybe one of the crocodiles would be better—could swallow him in one big gulp. That would definitely mean she could put the whole thing behind her.

Ana stretched as she jumped down from the truck, trying to uncurl the kinks and soften up the tension that was rampant in every one of her muscles. Another night, another tent pitch—after three weeks of wrestling with the canvas she was a bit over it.

Bundy walked over. 'You two will want to share a tent.'

What? Ana turned and found Seb right beside her. Every muscle seized again. Why on earth would Bundy think that?

'Yeah.' Seb answered before she managed to breathe, let alone think.

'Set up just beyond that tree over there. That way you'll get a little privacy.' He winked.

Ana gaped.

'Thanks,' Seb said.

It was one of those all-bloke moments where there was nothing for her to do but turn her back and pretend that that grin swap between the two men hadn't happened. That she wasn't going crimson with embarrassment.

No. It was rage.

Seb pulled a tent bag from the pile and went over to where Bundy had indicated. Ana stomped after him. Privacy was indeed necessary because she was about to commit first-degree murder.

'Why does he think we'd want to share a tent?' She just managed not to shout.

'I told him we're married.'

'What? Why?'

'Well, we are. It was how I could get on the truck at this late stage.'

So Bundy thought it was going to be some happy reunion? She narrowed her glare. 'I thought you said our meeting on the truck was a coincidence.'

He grinned. 'I lied.'

She whirled on him quick smart. 'Not for the first time, Seb.' Oh, yes, in with the knife.

But he just smiled wider with appreciation. 'I underestimated how good it would be to see you too, Ana.'

As if this were good? She'd never planned to see Seb again. And she certainly wasn't going to spend a night in a tent with him. Prickling heat washed from her scalp down. The only person who'd known where she'd gone was Phil. She was totally having words with him when she got back to London.

Irritated, she watched how quickly Seb assessed

the tent parts lying in a heap where he'd tipped them out. Yeah, it wouldn't take him the best part of an hour to figure it out first time as it had her. She hated how tiny the school-camp-like pup tents were. It had been almost bearable when she'd been on her own. But with Seb? She was just over six feet. He wasn't far off six and a half. Neither of them could sleep in there without curling up and they both couldn't do that in there unless they curled up *together*. She wouldn't be able to breathe. She couldn't breathe now when she was in one of the widest open spaces in the world and he was two metres away.

Because it was still there, wasn't it? Despite everything, despite all that had happened, she still wanted him. One look—*at the back of him*—and it had started again. The heightened awareness, the senses that had been dormant for so long were now switched on and scurrying for attention, craving touch—his.

She rebelled. 'I'm not sharing a tent with you, Seb.'

'We have to.'

'No, we do not.'

He shrugged, a hint of apology in his eyes. 'Bundy said there weren't any spare tents.'

'Then you can sleep in a mosquito net under the stars.' Or in the truck. Or in with the snakes. Anywhere, but not near her. 'I've got one you can use.'

'OK.' He held her gaze and softly repeated her words. 'Under the stars.'

And suddenly she remembered another time when he'd suggested just that. Another dark, wide sky. There'd been no net, no sheets, nothing but warm naked bodies. Their wedding night. On their balcony in Gibraltar and she'd been blinded by those stars.

Ana felt the flush slither across her skin like a nest of snakes disturbed and sliding out in all directions. She bent and started spreading out the tent totally haphazardly.

'Look, let me do it.' Seb pushed her out of the way. 'Why don't you go get a drink or something? You look all hot and bothered.'

'I can manage.' Didn't he realise she'd been doing just that for months now?

'I'm sure you can,' he said. 'But I haven't been sitting under the sun for days on that truck. Go and have a minute in the shade.'

She was perfectly capable of pitching the tent. But she wasn't stupid. He wanted to pitch the tent for her? Fabulous. She might as well get some kind of positive out of this. 'Thanks.'

She was hot. And breathless. She took the sarong she used as a towel and headed to the bathroom. Cold showers were all there were at campsites like this. And they were wonderful.

Afterwards she wandered off to where the animals were housed. Stared for an age at the big crocodile basking in the sun, lying so still he looked as if he were carved from stone.

'Do you think he's actually alive?' Seb asked.

'Don't be fooled,' she answered, not turning to face him, not surprised that he'd found her. 'He can move faster than you can blink.'

The snakes didn't appeal to her, looking at her with their cold and dangerous eyes, but she was fascinated by the chameleon. She stood watching his eyes swivel in all directions at once, amazed by the speckles of bright colour on his skin.

'He can't decide what his camouflage should be.' Seb chuckled.

She could relate to the poor thing, didn't know which way to defend herself against her own weakness. But as she watched the lizard she couldn't stop curiosity from biting.

'So what about you, Seb? Why are you travelling alone? Is there no one to warm your sleeping bag?'

'You can if you want.' He laughed outright at her look. 'Well, you asked.' He rubbed his knuckle against the stubble of his jaw and a hint of rue flickered in his eye. 'Actually it's been a long time since I even kissed someone.'

She turned from the chameleon. 'You expect me to believe that?'

'Well, yes.'

She rolled her eyes. 'Sebastian, I've been with you. I know what you're like.' She knew exactly his potency—his ability to move far faster than that crocodile ever could.

'I haven't been with anyone since you. What happened between us wasn't normal, Ana.'

'No.' She managed a smile. It certainly wasn't for her.

'I don't usually ask women to marry me.'

She laughed. 'Has the experience put you off all women for good, Seb?' Wouldn't that just have served him right?

Coolly he held her gaze. 'Perhaps.'

Wow—there wasn't a hint of jest in his tone.

'Have you met anyone else?' he asked.

'Not that many men like a woman who towers above them.'

'You don't tower. I'm taller than you.'

'You're not most men.'

His gaze dropped, she felt his focus skim over her as if it were his hand. 'Most men love long legs.'

She shook her head—he was so wrong. 'Most men run a mile.' He still looked so disbelieving she got cross. 'It's OK for you. You're a man. It's an asset. For a woman to be as tall as I am? It's freak status. I see them, Seb, staring, laughing, coming up to stand behind me at the bar, measuring themselves against the giant woman.'

His brows contracted. 'It really bothers you? But they only stare because you're beautiful.'

Yeah, right.

He stepped closer. 'There's really been no one else?'

Was that all he cared about? 'No,' she answered, unable to lie or to stop her own huskiness. 'But that's irrelevant, Seb.'

He glanced back to the chameleon. 'Maybe.'

She wasn't going to let him confuse her. She wasn't going to allow the past to rear up and toss her off course again—not now she was finally on top of it.

She turned to walk back to the safety of the others. But Seb moved, standing in front of her, not touching her, yet not letting her pass by. She looked up at him, trying to make her lack of interest plain. A little difficult, though, given that her body was determined to be interested.

He almost smiled. But his eyes were too sharp and his body too tense.

'Dinner will be ready.' She broke the taut silence with a voice almost too husky to be heard. 'I'm starving.'

* * *

She ate quietly, listened to Seb chatting to the others. He offered no reason for his appearance, didn't explain their relationship and thankfully everyone was too polite to ask. But she could see them warming to him just as everyone who came in contact with him did. She had—so had Phil—when they'd been out on the town that night. It was impossible not to be charmed by the smile, the attentiveness, the goddamn brilliant social skills. They were out in play tonight. She could see the boys thinking he was a good guy and the girls giving her sideways looks as if they were wondering how the hell she got so lucky.

If only they knew. The kind of warm attentiveness he showed here was nothing on the focus he showed in bed. Her cheeks burned with fast-flying provocative memories. It was as if he dedicated every bit of himself to the art of pleasure—time and time again. She'd thought it would be endless.

She shifted. Went and did the dishes even though it wasn't her turn on the roster. She just couldn't sit still, couldn't be near him.

The darkness was swift and complete. And even though there were millions of stars they were miles away and threw no light on the ground. She wouldn't sleep in the open air here—there were too many scary things about like snakes and scorpions and, heaven forbid, lions. But Seb was big and strong and would just have to handle it. In the tent she curled up in her tee shirt and tried not to feel guilty.

Hours later, still awake, she heard the splotch, splotch, splotch. Recognised it immediately and registered the quickening tempo. It hadn't rained often on her trip, but when it rained, it really rained. It only took

three of the super-sized drops and you were saturated.
She shut her eyes and cursed the weather gods. But not
even she could leave him out there to drown in warm
mud.

She flicked on her torch and unzipped the canvas.
'Seb. Get in here.'

He was only a few yards away and already sitting
up, muttering beneath his breath.

'Come on, hurry up.'

He was in sooner than she would ever be ready for.
His big frame took up the bulk of the space and he
stuffed his sleeping sheet in too.

'Damn.' With one swift movement he whipped his
shirt up over his head.

'What are you doing?'

He tossed the tee into the corner. 'What does it
look like?'

'You're...' Oh, my. He was amazing. She remembered the muscles—back then she'd been amazed too,
had wondered how a man who spent so much of his
life in a suit got muscles like those. But now he was
even leaner, his body even more defined. The six-pack
was rock-hard and her fingertips begged to trace the
shape of the muscles in his arms.

'Taking off my wet clothes, yes.'

He was undoing his shorts, his big hands working
smoothly. She remembered the feel of them on her.
How close he'd pulled her to him. The heat of the night
and the beat of the music. The madness that had swept
over her, making her sigh yes, yes, yes.

'You know there are scorpions around—you might
get bitten,' she snapped.

He looked amused, took his time about peeling off his

shorts and revealing the brief boxers beneath. 'I might get bitten by something a lot bigger than one of those.'

She flicked the torch off.

'Hey.' He reached across and flicked it back on. 'I want to find my sleeping bag, you know.' He chuckled. 'You wouldn't want me making a mistake and getting into the wrong one, would you?'

She looked at the way his eyes were dancing; the old Seb shone out at her—the joker, the tease. He made it too easy, so much fun. Oh, yeah, she and every other woman on the planet could do nothing but say yes to that smiling good humour.

She curled her legs up under her big sloppy tee and dived into the silk liner of her sleeping bag. Boiling already.

As she stared up at the roof of the tent, her legs drawn up, the silence was agony. She could hear every rustle. Her own breathing was too loud, too fractured. How the hell was she going to sleep when her whole body was wired? It was as if he was this great source of power that made her hum when he got within ten feet. Now within one foot she was just about floating off the ground hoodoo-voodoo style.

She closed her eyes and counted as she breathed, trying to think of something—anything—but him. But as the rain pelted down the futility of it got to her and she started to laugh. Once she started, she couldn't stop.

And he laughed too. Deep and rich and loud. That wonderful warm sound sliced through her tension, freeing her to feel a weird kind of relief. She loved the sound of his laughter.

And then suddenly she was filled with tension

again. That stupid yearning as she remembered hours of rolling and laughing with him in what she'd thought had been the affair of a lifetime.

She sobered completely. 'Did you have to come all the way to Africa, Seb?'

'Yeah,' he sighed, sounding as if he regretted it as much as she. 'I did.'

CHAPTER THREE

WHEN Ana opened her eyes Seb was sprawled next to her, taking up far too much of the tent to be fair. She was cramped up between him and the top of her pack. And from the sound of his regular breathing, he was still asleep. Carefully she rolled towards him, leaned a fraction closer to study his face in a way she wouldn't dare when he was conscious and could catch her. But stealing a look now could do no harm.

Wrong, because there was his scent, curling around her—the suddenly familiar heady scent of Seb. How could she have forgotten that? Her heart thumped in her chest. Tension mixed with something else as she remembered sensations she'd forced from her memory months ago. He had stubble on his jaw—she remembered the feel of that beneath her fingers, tickling her stomach, gently abrading her upper thighs…

She breathed out. Don't go there—

But his lips were full and she remembered how they'd felt, how they'd drawn everything from her. She looked down from them. His chest was free of the silk sleeping liner, his shoulders broad and bared and so incredibly muscular. Every cell in her tightened at the sight. He was still the most handsome man she'd ever known.

'Ana.' It was the tiniest whisper but the husky note plucked deep within her.

Slowly she turned her attention from his torso to his eyes. A hint of drowsiness lingered, but something else glinted in their depths. A seriousness. He knew she'd been looking—all too hungrily.

For an instant neither moved.

'I'm on breakfast duty.' She was too close. Her fault. She yanked on her shorts and grabbed her bikini top. She'd slip it on under the sloppy tee behind a tree or something. Just as he sat up she escaped, ignoring him when he called her name again.

But she trembled as those senses she had thought had been dulled roared back into life: sight, smell, sound, touch.

Taste. She ached to taste.

How could she still want to? How could she when she knew getting close like that before had meant nothing to him and everything to her? When she'd been through something so terrible because of her affair with him? How was it possible?

But her body wasn't listening to her brain, wasn't interested in those memories. No, the muscles were remembering something else. The weight, the sensation, the pleasure that his body had pulled from hers haunted her now. Her body yearned for it again. Uncaring of what the consequences had been before.

She walked to the heart of the campsite where Bundy already had the fire going and the billy boiling. She poured a cup of tea and drank it hot and black, wincing at the burn on her lips and the roof of her

mouth. The superficial pain was a good reminder—
that she didn't need any more of the real kind.

Breakfast was over in a rush. She didn't look at Seb.
Her muttered 'thanks' barely audible when she saw
he'd packed up the tent and had her pack ready alongside his.

The Jeeps arrived to take them to the rim of the
Ngorohgoro Crater. She jumped up from the grass
and walked towards them, but Seb was beside her
before she'd taken two paces. His eyes danced as he
tossed everything of theirs into the back.

Ana fidgeted, longing to fall back on her old
defence—to run. But here there was no escape—not
when he held the door and then climbed in right beside
her.

The road was the most appalling surface she'd ever
been on. Craters instead of tracks, cavernous potholes,
mud dried harder than concrete all combined to jerk
the Jeep from side to side and had them all suspended
in the air above their seats several times. Seb simply
reached up above and held onto the frame of the Jeep,
and put his other arm around Ana, pulling her into his
side, steadying her. But she'd have been better off
bumping against the steel frame, because he felt
harder, more solid than any metal framing.

Finally they got to the campsite near the top of
the crater rim. The Jeep pulled up and they spilled
out. Tomorrow they'd go in and see the wildlife. Ana
could hardly wait—she had some live lion feed to
toss over the side.

Seb stretched the cramps out and watched Ana walk
a distance towards the lounge facility. He couldn't

stop walking after her as he saw her take off her tee shirt. Wearing just a bikini top, with low-slung cotton shorts, her incredible body was open to view. How could she possibly think those legs were too long?

He lengthened his strides, took them faster, reached for her arm and turned her. Her cheeks were lightly flushed. The blue of her eyes shone bright and deep and she watched him as slowly, deliberately, he looked down her length.

'What is that?' He cleared his throat. Hadn't realised he was hoarse.

'What?'

He pointed a finger at her belly button. 'That.'

'Oh.'

He watched with masculine pleasure as the colour deepened under the skin of her cheeks. 'A navel piercing.'

Yeah, he knew that, but it felt damn good to see her react to him like that—knowing she still felt something too. Because his body was going out of control. 'When?'

'A few months ago.'

'Why?'

She looked about to roll her eyes like some sulky teen caught out using peroxide for the first time. 'It was a suggestion in a self-help book. Do something out of character—like get a tattoo or a piercing. I went for the non-permanent option.'

'You did it because a book said to?' He wanted to laugh but he was too busy staring. 'What sort of a book is that?'

'Quite a good one, actually.'

'So you're empowered now?'

'Assertive.'

He did laugh then, for just a second. Ana was assertive? As if. Then he sobered and couldn't resist touching. He pressed his hand flat to her belly, the navel ring centred between his thumb and forefinger. He felt her muscles quiver, felt the warmth of her skin. Felt the need for her bite harder. 'Did it hurt?'

He lifted his gaze for her reply.

'No.' The challenge was back in her voice. 'I've been through worse.'

The blue of her eyes was incredibly deep—ultramarine—and way too easy to drown in. And he was so close to kissing her.

If she was assertive, as she reckoned, he'd probably get a slap for it. And he deserved it, didn't he? Because she'd taken their marriage seriously when he'd intended it to be a fun fling, never a forever kind of deal. He'd thought it was obvious, a holiday romance on steroids, but looking back he knew they'd been too busy sleeping together instead of talking about what they actually wanted. And still he wanted to sleep with her. The fire still burned—even now, months after she'd walked out.

'Uh.' He scrambled for words, any kind of coherent thought so he wouldn't make a fool of himself. 'What did your mum say?'

She blinked, obviously surprised. 'About the navel ring? Seb,' she laughed—a humourless choke. 'My mum's dead.'

It was Seb's turn to blink. Was that a recent thing? He'd had no idea. 'Hell, Ana, I'm sorry.'

'It's OK. It was a long time ago.'

'Oh.' He matched her small smile and aimed to lighten. 'So what did your dad say?'

Her smile faded. He should have known better—total foot-in-mouth syndrome.

'They died together in an accident, Seb. I was six.'

Seb sucked in a breath. 'Ana, that's terrible.'

She stepped back, was going to walk away. But he didn't want her to walk away. He wanted to know now—ask all the questions he hadn't bothered with before. Maybe then he could understand her more. And his hand was cold now it wasn't touching her. 'Who did you go to, then?'

'My mother's brother and his wife.'

Seb walked slowly beside her, wary about asking the obvious but unable to resist. 'Are they nice?'

She stopped walking. 'You really want to know, Seb?'

He nodded.

She shook her head. 'I was the stereotypical lonely orphan. They already had two children of their own—perfect little blonde things. I just didn't fit in. Could never make the grade. And I was grieving. I guess I made it difficult for them right from the start. I closed up. I was hard work.'

She was smiling, a touch of sarcasm acting as cover-up, but Seb got the glimpse of a pain that just had to run deep. 'You were six. You had a right to grieve. You were lost. They should have found you.'

She should have been brought safely home. And Seb understood what it was not to be wanted—hadn't he had that vibe from a step-parent or two? 'Did it get better? Did you get on with your cousins?'

'Not really.'

It had got worse, huh?

'I left home as soon as I could.'

Definitely worse.

'What about you? You have brothers and sisters?'

Seb hesitated. Where to begin on any of that nightmare? Yeah, he knew how hard it was to try to get along with other kids you had nothing in common with but that you had to live with because of the adults in your life. In his case it was because of the marriages—and remarriages— of his parents. But that was too big a can of worms and he went for the easy option. 'No.' He looked at her, waited for her to look at him. 'Jeez, we really didn't know each other at all, did we?'

She held his gaze for a moment. Then laughed and turned away. 'I don't think we wanted to. I think we were both too happy in our own la-la lands.'

He laughed at that. It was true. It had been such madness. 'But it was good, wasn't it?' He couldn't resist pointing it out. 'What we did have.'

There was a slight rise of her shoulders—and a total avoidance of answer. As a result he was compelled by the need to press her for more. 'So why did you come to Africa? Did you send the divorce papers and then run away?' That was a talent of hers, wasn't it—running away?

'I didn't run away. I wanted an adventure. One that I was in control of.'

As opposed to the adventure they'd had together? The one in which neither of them had been in control? 'Were you going to see me when you got back?'

'No.'

She'd sent him the divorce papers, a brief note outlining her plans and asking for the paperwork to be sent to her new lawyer. She hadn't wanted to see him;

she'd hoped he'd simply sign and send it all away. 'You're a coward, Ana.'

She was silent for a moment. Then he saw her chin go up. 'I was. For a long time I was,' she agreed quietly. 'But I'm not any more.'

Ana spent the late afternoon reading in the shade and ignoring the football game Seb had organised amongst the lads. She didn't need reminding of how fit he was. She was already spending far too much time thinking of his incredible sex drive.

But at dinner he sat beside her and made her converse—asked her about other highlights of the Africa trip, about what she'd seen and done. Safe topics. And yet not safe—because it was so easy to smile, to laugh, to relax. And as darkness swooped the conversation lengthened, deepened until she lost track of time.

She didn't sleep much through the night—conscious of him lying only yards away outside. She woke early, hot and bothered, and sat inside the tent to control her hormones and fast-beating heart. It wasn't just his physical proximity, it was the talking-with-him thing too. It made him all the more attractive. What she needed was some confidence. Some 'don't think you can mess with me' attitude. She delved deep into the bottom of her pack and resolutely strapped on the ridiculous shoes she'd lugged round for weeks. She couldn't believe she'd brought them with her, nor that she was actually going to wear them now. But it was a desperate situation. Something about Seb made her want to have the guts to wear them and get away with it. He thought she wasn't too tall? She'd show him.

He noticed them right away. 'Oh, they're so appropriate, aren't they? High heels on safari.'

'Yes, they are.' She took up the challenge. 'You don't like how tall they make me?'

He shrugged, arrogantly uncaring. 'I'm still taller than you.'

Her eyes narrowed. 'One day I'll find a pair that'll make me taller than you.'

'Try the circus—they have stilts there.'

'You're not afraid of looking up to me?'

'Your height doesn't intimidate me.' He grinned. 'It's actually quite interesting.' He leaned and dropped his voice to seduction volume. 'A good fit where it counts. No need for me to be a contortionist.'

Oh, now there was a thought. It was too easy to go over the line with him. And she went one further, provocatively leaning closer, a mere millimetre from contact, registering with pleasure the widening of his eyes. 'Want to know the best thing about these shoes?'

His mouth opened but no sound emerged.

She smiled. 'The heels are really good for treading on toes when someone gets too close.' She pulled back and flicked a cool look at him.

His eyes narrowed. 'I consider myself warned.'

'Great.' She turned and positively strutted away, hiding the grin of victory.

They climbed back into the Jeeps and drove down the rocky road into the crater—one of the world's natural heritage sites. It was a trip she'd been looking forward to for ages and despite only a few hours' broken sleep she was determined to make the most of it—damned if she was going to let her chaotic hormones ruin it.

They drove onto the floor of the crater, stood up in the roofless Jeep to get a better view of the abundance of animals. In the magnificence she forgot her fight with him—and herself.

'What's your inner beast, Seb? Lion? Oh, no, I know.' She smiled sweetly. 'Cheetah.'

He shot her a look. 'No. Elephant.'

'What,' she asked innocently, 'because of your big trunk?'

'Thanks for the compliment, sweetheart, but no. My memory. I might not have known much about you, Ana, but what I did learn I've never forgotten.' He leaned and whispered into her ear. 'I remember what you like. I remember how you like it—how fast, how deep, how often.'

Desire gushed into her belly at his boldness. Knew it was payback for her heeled-shoes moment.

'You know what kind of animal you are?' He tucked a strand of hair behind her ear.

'Don't you dare say giraffe.' She reminded herself to breathe.

'Wouldn't dream of it.' His eyes gleamed. 'I was thinking more along the lines of a gazelle.'

And she was in trouble again when he looked at her like that. 'You've got to be kidding.' She *was* a giraffe—all tall angles and gangly. Not remotely like one of those nimble, petite, pretty things.

'No, I mean it. Jumpy.' He seemed to be closer still. 'Skittish. Takes fright.'

'I don't take fright.' She inched back further against the hard railing of the Jeep.

'Yes, you do,' he said softly. 'That's OK. I'm patient enough to stalk my prey.'

She refused to be his prey. 'Elephants are vege-tarians.'

'Well, then, I guess I must really be a lion.'

Ana lifted her chin. 'Actually more often it's the lioness who hunts.'

'Really? Go on, then,' he murmured. 'Show me your claws.'

She pulled the last millimetre she could away.

'See. I was right first time.' Somehow he took up even more of the cramped space. 'A little, jumpy gazelle.'

She sucked her tummy in and spun on the spot, turned her back to him to lean forward over the rail, determinedly focused on the view. No more verbal sparring—he always seemed to win.

She breathed in the sights: the flamingos in the distance on the lake, the hippos hanging out in the water, the hyenas creepily stalking around. And he seemed to let it lie. Pointed out shots for her, took pictures of her. Grinned with her when they found the lion, stretched in the shade, who didn't seem to care about the humans standing up in the open-topped Jeep with their cameras clicking like crazed paparazzi. She couldn't believe she was so close to it, and her heart stopped completely when a cub came into view with its mother.

'Look, Seb!' she whispered, turning to make sure he'd seen.

He wasn't looking at the animals. He was looking at her with the fierce stillness and concentration of a hunter. But it wasn't the animals in danger.

'Are you taking anti-malaria pills?' she asked curtly. 'I'm thinking you might be running a fever or something. You have this glazed look.'

He reached out and put the back of his hand against her brow. 'But you're the one looking hot.'

She ducked back out of the way. 'There's no cure for you, is there?'

He grimaced. 'Apparently not.'

Seb sat squashed up to her for all the horrendous drive past the campsite of the previous night, and all the way back to the snake park where the truck was waiting. Hours of driving and having his length pressed to her. The frustration was going to be the death of him. Hard up against his body he could feel each ragged inhalation as she tried to regulate her breathing. She strained back from him. Looking down, he could see the outline of her nipples pointing up at him through the thin stretchy bikini top. He could see every little indentation of what he knew were deliciously large areolae, and the tight hard nubs that he ached to nibble on.

Desire surged through him, it had been so damn long. And he knew she felt it too—they were dancing around it, moving ever closer with words and looks.

But they weren't suited. He'd never forget the hurt in her face when she'd asked him if he'd only married her to get his partnership. What had he thought? That it was true love? OK, yeah, she had thought that. But while they'd been having a wild and fabulous fling, that was all it was. He'd been blinded by lust—both for her and for his promotion—and the marriage had just been an opportunity to secure them—for a while at least. But as if he really believed in it? He spent his life finalising the end for so many marriages she couldn't have thought he'd meant it—it had been for his work. And his own parents had taught him time and time again how easily such vows were broken and forgotten. But she hadn't known about that, had she? He hadn't told her a thing about himself.

And the one thing he couldn't forget now was the feel of her. He tumbled out of the Jeep and walked to the truck to get a drink. Cool himself down from the inside out before he tried to burn more of the bloody frustration with some football. But there was no way in hell football could burn off the energy in his body.

Ana assembled the tent in record time, desperate to build herself a hidey-hole even if for only a few minutes. Quickly she crawled inside and then zipped up the flap. She breathed hard, sweating. A day jammed up hard next to Sebastian without actually having him was enough to exhaust any woman. Her insides were all shook up and it wasn't from the bumpy road. She stared at the faded green tent fabric. Despite the tiredness, sleep felt miles away. Memories and words, both said and unsaid, spun round and round in her brain like a mad merry-go-round.

She ached to shut it down; even more she ached to be able to switch off the 'on' button that Seb's mere presence had fired. As if Africa weren't hot enough? Why did he have to come along and up the mercury another thirty degrees or so with his soft touches and all-seeing eyes? Every tiny touch made her skin spark and now she *ached*.

Sweat that had gathered at the base of her hairline trickled in an irritatingly slow way down her neck, eventually pooling between her breasts—breasts that felt big and heavy and tender. She longed for a shower—

for cool water endlessly gushing from a gleaming chrome head. The fantasy was almost as good as the other one playing in the back of her mind—the one where she wasn't getting cooler but hotter and the source of the spike wasn't a shower or a spa but one potent man.

Neither were achievable options right now. OK, so she could go have a shower, but that would mean walking out in public—past the footballers—and she was too wobbly. But she did have one luxury. Wet wipes. The best thing she'd brought with her to Africa. She'd use a few—give herself a sponge bath with the delicately scented, blessedly cool wipes.

She undid her bikini top and peeled it from her sticky body. Popped the plastic lid and pulled some of the small white squares from the container. She sat cross-legged on the groundsheet and closed her eyes, simple relief sweeping her as she slid the damp tissues over her too hot, too sensitive skin.

The buzzing sound was loud and fast. She froze mid-swipe. Suddenly moved to pick up her top but he moved faster—his hand grasping hers, holding it out away from her bared body. With his other hand he quickly slid the zip down behind him, sealing them in the tent.

'I thought you were going to play football,' she said quickly.

'I… needed…to get…' He took his time answering.

Eventually she prompted, 'Get what?'

'I don't know.' His eyes were wide and filled with fire.

'Sebastian.' She tried to shake her head but the heat washed over her, melting her ability to move.

He didn't look as if he'd heard anyway. The hunger in his gaze fired an equal hunger deep within her. Her nipples budded—practically screamed for his touch—tight and hard. Her breasts were heavy and full. Despite everything she wanted him to reach out to her, to cup them, to kiss them. To relieve the agonising torment that was this desire.

The muscles in his jaw worked as he clenched his teeth. Slowly his eyes lifted to meet hers. The fever burned between them. She heard the low growl as he turned and got out of the tent faster than a striking snake.

Ana tipped right over where she was, planting her face in the soft, suffocating sleeping bag. What the hell was she doing? She pulled on a new sloppy tee and went out. He was far away from the others viciously kicking a ball at a tree, hitting it with unerring precision. Time and time again. She walked over to him.

He glanced at her and immediately away. 'Don't come near me now.'

She halted. 'Why not?'

'Because I want to kiss you. I want to do more than kiss you.'

Thwack. The ball hit the tree again. And her legs could hardly hold her up.

'You have no idea what I want to do to you,' he muttered. Fists clenched, muscles bulging, his bare torso shone with sweat. He was primed.

Heat flooded in her most secret places. And she was the one panting like the one doing the crazy workout in the heat of the afternoon.

He stopped, stood with his hands on his hips and

glared at her. 'We started something back then, Ana. And for me it isn't over. I thought it was. But it isn't.' He gave the ball a mighty kick. 'But I don't want to mess either of us around again. So don't come near me.'

CHAPTER FOUR

EVERY time Ana looked up Seb was looking at her. The odd moments he was talking to someone else she watched him. Invariably he caught her at it, as she did him. Their eyes simply wouldn't stray from each other for too long. It wasn't a thread between them, it was a big, thick rope winding tighter and tighter.

Sexual attraction was blind to the faults of each individual, didn't care how mismatched the two were. It was pure chemistry that couldn't be denied. But hopefully it could be ignored.

She tried to put distance between them—sat up on the exposed frame of the truck, ostensibly to get a better view of the landscape. But the metal crossbars got too hard for her butt and she had no choice but to sit on the seat in the truck again.

And in the end she obeyed her body's demand and took the seat next to his.

He might have told her to stay away but she found it impossible. They were in such close confines and she found herself in orbit circling closer and closer to his heat.

And all the while her mind searched to rationalise

it. They were on the long drive through to Dar Es Saleem, on a truck with twelve other people. Nothing could happen, and so the closeness was safe.

He spoke almost as soon as she sat. 'Tell me about this business of yours.'

She nodded. Good idea. They could talk personal, but not intimate. 'It's a rental business.'

'Renting what—washing machines? Driers? DVDs?'

'Accessories.'

'Computer accessories? What?'

'Fashion accessories.' She wasn't surprised at his look and tried to explain it further. 'What does the fairy godmother say in *Cinderella*?'

'Be back by midnight?'

'Bibbity Bobbity Bo. That's what she says and, *voilà*, Cinderella is transformed. Well, my idea is Bibbity-Bobbity-*Bling*. I'm the godmother you come to when you need glitz and glam, or stylish and label but you can't afford to buy it yourself.' She started to laugh. 'Do you know, I have so many trinkets, millions of high-heeled sparkly shoes and bags like you wouldn't believe.'

Seb twisted in his seat and angled his head at her. 'Don't take this the wrong way, Ana, but you don't strike me as a fashionista.'

'I know,' she sighed. 'I'm a total wannabe. Or I was. Do you know I spent every cent of my student loan and ran up a hu-u-uge credit-card debt buying shoes and bags and *stuff*? But do you want to know the really stupid thing?' She laughed again at her ridiculousness. 'I never had the guts to wear it. It's all pristine in bags and yet I still can't bear to part with it.'

She shook her head. She'd wanted to be feminine

and gorgeous but she'd been so stuck in her 'black, melt into the shadows' phase she hadn't been able to break free of it and she'd been mad. It had been like a kind of addiction. She hadn't comfort eaten, she'd comfort shopped.

'It took so long to pay off the debt and I screwed my credit rating.' She had cleared the debt—a couple of years of working two or three jobs—and she had no intention of getting into debt ever again. 'And instead of having all these quirky, stylish pieces sitting gathering dust, I need to turn them around and make them work for me. So I'm going to add a bit to my stock and make them for hire. I've got the website planned and half built. I'm looking for premises but still deciding quite where.' She stopped for breath, realised she'd been gabbling. 'Do you think it's stupid?'

'No.' He looked a little dazed. 'I think it could work. It really could.'

She knew it could. Because she was sure there were women out there like her who wanted but couldn't afford, and wasn't it better to hire than buy something you weren't going to be using daily—these were not things anyone really *needed*. But it was about being able to have some fun. She wanted the fun.

'The shoes you were wearing in the crater—'

'Yeah. They're some.'

He laughed.

She laughed too. 'I know it's mad.'

'What made you wear them yesterday?'

She shrugged. Not wanting to admit it had been because of him.

'You should wear them more.'

She couldn't stop her smile then. 'I've got some with even higher heels.'

'No way.'

She nodded and told him of some of her other insane purchases. Loved his grin, loved his questions and his belief in the idea. They talked for hours, halfway through the night. Until everyone around them was asleep except poor Bundy driving in the cab in the front.

And then they didn't talk any more. There was just that slow burning awareness as the truck drove on, the noise of the engine rough and loud in the wide, still night. Eventually she moved—forced herself to get away. Lay on the bagged tents that had been stacked in the aisle and stretched out—the most comfortable spot on the truck. The tarpaulin roof was still pulled back and she had the most incredible view of the stars, watching the lights that were moving—satellites or space junk or something. It was so dark she could barely make out the shadow of the other passengers. But of one thing she was certain. He was watching her.

Man, it was hot—since the second the sun had started to rise its power had been extreme. It didn't help that Seb was now sitting in the seat next to the aisle and Ana's long tanned legs were swinging down beside him from where she was perched back up on the cross-bars that supported the tarpaulin covering. The drive through the night had nearly been the death of him. While he'd enjoyed how they'd talked, he wished like hell they'd been alone—or were alone now. Then he'd tug on that delectably fine-boned ankle and pull her down, kiss her as he'd been dreaming of kissing her for days. Watching her rest on the bagged tents in the wee small hours, he'd fantasised about the kind of mattress they'd make if only they were alone. If only she'd say yes. If only they weren't bloody married and had enough mess between them already.

The frustration was driving him crazy. There had been no one since her. And now he realised he wanted no one but her. But it would be beyond stupid. They'd muddied their lives enough with what they'd done the last time they'd given into temptation. They wanted different things—she wanted the whole happy-ever-after commitment bit and he just wanted fun and carefree. Problem was he only wanted to do fun with her.

Dar es Salaam came into view. Finally. Big and busy and when would the damn boat arrive to take them to Zanzibar? Seb was over the whole budget tourist thing. Of course he could stop here—ditch the truck and its passengers and go on his own road. But he couldn't bring himself to. Not now the fire had been lit in him once more. He'd remain a slave to temptation—bitten by the bug. He was enjoying her company too much to walk away just yet. And there was that hint of hope, wasn't there? He could see that look in her eye. So he couldn't leave.

It felt like for ever but finally Ana got off the boat and onto the island of Zanzibar. She needed to rest. The lack of sleep she'd had last night was messing with her reason and she was thinking things she really shouldn't.

Tempting things. Wicked things.

Ever since he'd told her to stay away she'd felt the desire to do the exact opposite. So she climbed into the waiting Jeep, moved along so he could sit beside her and they were taken away from the bustling Stone Town to one of the beaches on the far side of Zanzibar.

There were four bandas—huts—in a row and then another four behind those. The rest of the budget resort consisted of a large open-air bar/restaurant and an open-top toilet and shower facility. Basic at best. But so incredibly beautiful.

She walked into the banda that had been assigned to her and Seb. An A-frame made of wood and palm, its only furniture four built-in cot-like beds—bare wooden frames with canvas stretching over them—hard and only a fraction wider than single beds. There was no floor, just soft sand underfoot. And a door made of the same mass of woven-together leaves.

She turned and found he was standing in the doorway behind her. The weather gods had smiled upon her and he'd been in the mosquito net under the stars outside her tent every night since that first. But their tents and nets were back on the truck in Dar es Salaam and now there was just this dim, spacious hut.

'I don't think we should share,' he said, arms folded across his chest. 'I'll see if there's room in anoth—'

'It's OK.' She avoided looking at him. They were adults. They could handle it.

Besides, there was no way they could both squash up on those cots. Not without being on top of each other. But, oh, didn't she want just that?

No.

She stepped back at the same time as he and they avoided each other all afternoon as if by tacit agreement. As the evening progressed they sat on opposite sides of the bar and joined in the conversation with the others. Ana didn't drink. Nor, she noted, did he. Too dangerous. Any hint of intoxication would see her will sliding from her. Temptation would be impossible to resist.

So she played it safer still, loitering in the bar until it was late, changed into her sleepwear in the bathroom facility. Left it long enough to be sure he'd be already tucked safely away.

She didn't look at him as she slid inside her thin silk sleeping bag.

'Goodnight, Ana.' He flicked the torch off.

'Night, Seb.'

The narrow cot creaked as she wriggled on it, bunching up her fleece jumper again, trying to push it into more of a comfy pillow. Seb muttered about the length of the hard little beds. Then silence.

Minutes that felt like hours later she knew he was still awake. Could feel the awareness swirling between them in the room. She counted sheep, thought happy thoughts, closed her eyes and consciously tried to relax all her muscles.

Failed.

There was nothing else for it. They were just going to have to do more of what they'd been too busy to do before.

Talk.

'Seb?'

'Mmm-hmm.'

'Are you awake?'

'Obviously.'

She grinned in the darkness and rolled onto her side to face him. 'Did you tell your parents you got married?'

'Hell, no,' he laughed.

'Why not?'

'Well, for one thing you walked out before I had the chance. And for another they have enough failed marriages between them not to need me adding to the tally.'

'Your parents are divorced?'

'Three times each. Mum is on her fourth marriage now. Dad'll no doubt play catch-up soon.'

Ana wished like hell she could see his face right now. 'You're kidding.'

'Would I make that up?'

Wow. What an experience. 'When did they divorce each other?'

He sighed. 'Do you really want to know this?'

'Yes.'

'They separated when I was twelve. Mum got married again that year. Dad the year after that. They both divorced again the year after that. To be honest, then I start to lose track.'

'What happened to you?'

'What do you mean what happened to me?' Defensive as ever there was.

'Who did you live with?'

'I split my time between them.'

Ana winced. She hadn't had the greatest home life—but at least it had been stable. One house, one lot of guardians. 'What were the step-parents like?'

'They varied.'

'Did you have stepbrothers or sisters?'

'Occasionally. For a while.' His answer was supposed to be a conversation closer.

But she ignored it, because that must have been

hard, because it explained just a little about him. 'But you don't have other siblings.'

'No.'

Utterly closed now and, as if to reinforce it, he pushed the questions onto her. 'What about you? How did your aunt and uncle take it?'

'I've never told them,' she said baldly, still thinking over his revelations.

'Really?' He grunted. 'When did you last see them?'

'Oh, I don't know. Over a year ago.'

'Over a year ago? As in before it happened?'

'Yeah.' She shrugged off his incredulity in the darkness. 'We're not close.'

'Obviously.' She could hear his frown. 'Things really were bad for you, weren't they?'

Oh, so he was thinking she had it worse than him now? Her heart lifted a notch. 'Not that bad, Seb. I was fed, clothed. But I just didn't fit in.' She hadn't been physically neglected, but she had been emotionally abandoned—and hurt. 'I wasn't what they wanted and I couldn't figure out how to be what they wanted.' She'd tried so hard for so long but it had never been enough. They hadn't wanted her, or loved her. 'We send the odd email.' She sighed. 'It wasn't their fault— they didn't ask to be landed with me. They did their best in a bad situation.'

'You're too generous. They should have loved to have you. They should have loved you.' There was a long pause. 'You were too generous with me, too.'

Why, because she'd wanted to give him her heart? Because she'd believed in the happy ever after? At least now his attitude towards it made more sense. He must have thought she was so naïve.

'I'm sorry I hurt you,' he said quietly.

She could actually smile and shake her head. 'It wasn't all your fault.' And it wasn't—some of what had happened could never have been predicted. 'I said yes, didn't I? If I hadn't been so foolish it wouldn't have happened at all.' She'd wanted to believe so badly that someone could love her—that someone could fall completely in love with her like that. Oh, yes, totally fairy tale. Totally naïve. But she looked back on it with less of the total cringe factor now. Because while it hadn't been love, there had been no denying the lust—there was still no denying the lust. 'You were like this pirate—swooping in and taking what you wanted.'

'Yeah, well, I've learned my lesson.'

And maybe he had. He certainly wasn't pushing for what he wanted now. Even though a tiny part of her wanted him to, the rest of her actually respected him for it.

She pondered what he'd told her, couldn't stop another question going into the personal. 'Is that why you do divorce cases? Because of your parents?'

'Partly. I'd always wanted to go into law, and dispute resolution seemed the natural specialty, seeing I had a lot of practice with it.'

Practice in dispute resolution? It must have been ugly with his folks.

He sighed. 'People need saving from themselves.'

'People like us, you mean,' she chuckled.

'Ugh.' She heard movement and something landed with precision on her face. 'Enough. Now go to sleep.'

It was his shirt. She scrunched it up and stuffed it under her head together with the fleece. Told herself she was happier purely because of the comfort factor, not that she was getting giddy on the delicious pheromones.

CHAPTER FIVE

ANA walked across the stretch of sand and looked to the horizon. The colour of the water was hypnotic and she felt her limbs go supple. Her falling for him again was as inevitable as the autumnal leaf falling to the ground. But this time she'd choose her landing spot. This time she would float herself down and not be buffeted about by the compelling force that was Sebastian Rentoul. This time, if there was to be a this time, it had to be on her terms.

She looked at the never-ending blue and knew what she wanted. And what she didn't want. She was a different person from the naïve romantic she'd been back then. She had strength born of experience. And for once she wanted to have things her way.

She turned back up the beach. Sebastian was already involved in his usual displacement activity—had rallied the lads for a game on the large expanse of sand that spread ahead of the littlest of dunes that sloped down to meet the water.

It was truck-tour passengers versus locals. Ana sat in one of the old deckchairs in the shade and watched for a while. Until her thrumming body could no longer keep still. She stared at the net strung between a tree and a pole. Beach volleyball. Now there was a way of burning some of her energy—she couldn't watch him play a moment longer, not when he was running bare-foot, bare-chested, clad only in shorts, his bronzed body gleaming in the hot sun.

She picked up a volleyball from behind the bar and went to the net, called to him as she went past the makeshift footy pitch. Instantly he walked from that game and came to her.

He looked at the net. 'You want to play?'

Legs apart, she twirled the ball in her hands and grinned. 'I should warn you—I'm quite good.'

'I play to win, Ana.' He met her challenge and then raised it. 'The question is, what are we playing for?'

She inhaled through parted lips. 'Not that.' At least, not yet.

'Then what?' His smile said it all.

'Well, it doesn't really matter because I'm going to beat you.' Ana pulled her tee shirt over her head, re-maining only in bikini top and short shorts, relishing the freedom from the bulky cotton, amused by Seb's change in expression—from teasing to burning. Two could play at the distraction game.

She went under the net to the other side and served the ball over. His concentration was immediate—as was hers. Annoyingly they were evenly matched—was there no sport he couldn't master? But the exertion of running to prevent the ball from landing on her side didn't exhaust the pent-up energy in her body. Indeed her aggression manifested as their duel progressed. Frustration grew—and he became her target. She no longer aimed to get the ball on his ground; she wanted it on his head—hard. She wanted to provoke—to see if the pirate still lurked beneath the surface. She walloped the ball over the net with a strong spike. Her height had made volleyball a natural choice at school. She'd tried basketball but hadn't liked the up-close confrontation and contact—having the net between her and her opponent was better.

But now the net was in the way.

Seb was no longer smiling. The volleys became longer, more intense. Ana had no idea what the score was. She didn't just want to win. She wanted to conquer.

There was some noise as another carload of people arrived and Seb turned his head to watch just as Ana was readying to serve the ball. She took advantage of his inattention and hit it over—*hard*.

The ball landed with a satisfyingly loud smack on his chest. He took a step back and swore.

Ana couldn't help the giggle.

But half a second later he was under the net and running for her.

'Volleyball's a non-contact sport,' she shrieked. Instinct told her to run but the last word was knocked out of her along with all her breath as he tackled. He went in low, his shoulder hard in her stomach; she crumpled. He tossed her straight up and over in the classic fireman's lift and kept running.

His arm was a hard band around her thighs and it wasn't comfortable as she bumped on his shoulder. 'You need to cool down.'

Within seconds he was splashing through the waves, tumbling her in. She went under. His arm slipped from her and she twisted, swimming underwater, stretching out her tension. The warm water washed the fight from her, seducing her with its deep blue saltiness. She opened her eyes and followed the way the light refracted, drawing lines on the golden sand beneath. She swam along their path for a while, deeper into the ocean. Until her lungs screamed for air and she could no longer deny the way the rest of her ached.

She pulled her feet under her and stood, looked around for him.

He suddenly surfaced alongside her. Tall, fast, all muscle, all attention. They stood waist deep and stared at each other.

His body gleamed as the droplets sheeted from his golden skin. His muscles were bunched from the exercise. His jaw was shadowed by the light stubble, even more chiselled by the way he was gritting his teeth. And while his eyes were hooded, his pupils were huge.

And she knew. As crazy as it was there was no longer a choice, no reason to fight it. She knew what she wanted. She took a step towards him. And then another.

He stood. Watching, not moving—except for his chest, which rose and fell fast. She heard him panting—more breathless than when he played football for hours in the midday heat. But he said nothing.

She took another two steps, until only an inch or so separated them. As she relentlessly searched his expression his gaze dropped as if he didn't want to see what it was she was thinking. She leant closer still. So she could feel his breath on her cheek, his heated body only a millimetre away. She dropped her head so her mouth hovered above his skin.

'Doing this again is a bad idea,' he muttered.

'A very bad idea,' she agreed, moving so her words were muffled against his shoulder. His salt was delicious, and so was his tiny groan. And her mouth parted wider, hungry for more.

'Crazy.' His lips brushed her forehead as he spoke.

'Stupid.' Her tongue touched his collarbone, tracing the ridge.

His breath gusted out. 'Foolish.'

His head rested on hers for a moment; she nudged closer.

'Mad.' She lifted her hands, placing them, oh, so carefully on his chest, felt his heart thundering.

'Absolutely insane.' He dropped the whisper into her ear.

She closed her eyes, angled her head to let him nuzzle the side of her neck. 'Irresistible,' she breathed. 'Inevitable.'

He froze. So did she. It was the moment. The decision would be made.

Had been made.

'Inevitable.' He lifted his head, looked right into her eyes. 'Are you sure?'

'Is there a choice?' she asked.

His hands lifted, his fingers sliding into her hair, holding her face up to his. 'There's always a choice.'

She tipped her head back further into his hold, deliberately letting her breasts press into his chest, her mouth part under his gaze. 'Just once.'

'For old times' sake?'

She shook her head slightly. 'I'm not the person I was back then.'

'Nor am I,' he answered, sounding so serious, yet

he seemed to be devouring her features. 'So it's a one-night stand?'

It would be fitting. 'That's all it ever should have been.'

He nodded. 'Our getting married was a mistake.'

'Huge.'

'It's not something I ever meant to do. I can't offer anything more than—'

'You're a good-time guy. I understand,' she interrupted. 'That's all I want.'

'But last time—'

'I was naïve. I mistook lust for love. I have it straight now.'

Still he hesitated.

Last time he had driven everything. And now he was holding back—despite the effort she could feel it was costing him. But his rigidity, his restraint only made her want him more. It was her turn to push it now. 'I just want you, Seb. As a lover. For one night. Nothing more.'

One night to indulge—and to expunge—the attraction. Maybe then she would be utterly free to move on. And now she didn't want to think—just wanted to feel.

He looked at her, eyes lingering on her lips. Lips that she licked—not to deliberately provoke or manipulate his response, but because they were so dry, felt so swollen with her fast-beating blood. He slid one hand round her waist, kept the other in her hair and pulled her closer against him.

She closed her eyes against the brilliance of the blue sky, the blue water.

And then she felt it—his lips on hers. Warm, salty

and yet so sweet. She felt his body leap harder and the passion that had simmered for so long boiled over.

They kissed, broke apart, kissed again. His fingers threaded more tightly in her hair, tilting her so he could kiss her jaw. She arched further, encouraging him to kiss down her neck. Moaned at the delight of the hot, fast caresses and the urgency with which he curved his hand around her bottom.

'Ana.'

She liquefied just with the way he muttered her name.

'Inside,' she breathed. 'I want…inside.' She wanted to be inside the hut; she wanted him inside.

Hands clinging to skin, they walked up the sand, went to their banda. Seb pulled the door closed behind them and secured the simple latch.

It was cooler inside, dim and suddenly silent.

He moved ahead, picked up his sleeping bag. The whirring was loud as he unzipped it. Then he tossed it wide so it floated open onto the sand creating a place for them to lie together.

'Do you have contraception?' Her voice was a mere thread.

He turned, speared her with an unflinching gaze. 'Yes.'

Of course he did. She blinked, refused to mind that he'd brought it. That he was always prepared. Instead she was glad—because now she had double the protection. Pregnancy was never happening to her again. But with her on the Pill and him with a condom, she would stay safe.

This would be sex purely for the pleasure. And no fear.

She wanted him so incredibly badly. In a step he was beside her, turning her towards him, seeming to read her mixed emotions—fleeting though they were.

The kiss was the lightest brush. So gentle, nothing like the wild passion she'd expected. It had always been so wild and fast between them before. But something had changed. Now it was as if he was savouring every single moment.

She kept her eyes closed, holding still as he slowly explored her mouth, the tip of his tongue tracing her lips before he moved to cover them with his own. So soft, so sweetly roving. His fingers slid down her neck, the tips stroking down her pulse point to her most sensitive skin. And his tongue swept into her as his fingers firmed, holding her face up to his.

She felt the heat inside her; no longer was it just her skin burning, but deep within her belly too she was warming—to softness, wetness, wanting. She shivered as he kissed down the length of her neck, nibbling the delicate skin.

'You have such a sensitive neck.' He tilted her chin higher with his fingers, getting greater exposure to the vulnerable, and, yes, super-sensitive stretch of her body.

Sensation rushed, overwhelming her. His near nudity, sheer size and closeness made her head spin. She couldn't quite believe he was here, touching her once more—certainly not so gently, so carefully. She locked her muscles, trying to stop her all-over-body shaking, but her legs weren't going to hold her up anymore.

His hands caught her round the waist; gently he lowered them both to the ground. And he set about slowly, so slowly touching every inch of her. Light hands trailed over her arms, working in symmetry; the tips of his fingers slid across her shoulders, along her collarbones to meet in the middle, and then continued a path down. And then his mouth joined the exploration.

He untied her bikini top, lifted it away and then cupped her breasts. She opened her eyes, saw the intensity in his as he held her—thumbs circling the jutting peaks as he gazed down her body. He was good. He was so good and she'd tried so hard to forget. But now the memories rushed, her muscles both slackened and strained—knowing the delight that was to follow. She shook as he took her hard nipple in his mouth. His tongue sluiced over the sensitive nub and he sucked more of her into his hot mouth and she couldn't contain the strangled sound of delight.

His hands dropped to her waist and he finished stripping her, slipping her shorts and bikini bottoms all the way down her legs. And although the last of her covering had been removed she now felt hotter than if she were unshaded out in the heat of the African sun.

He took the arches of her feet in sure, steady hands and pushed them wider apart, spreading her before slowly sliding his hands up her calves, to her knees and then even more slowly up her thighs. And his mouth, his full sensual mouth marked the way with kisses, his tongue accentuating each pleasurable pause.

And as he inched towards her core she moved, the tiniest rocking of her hips. She wanted him to get there. All the way to where she was wet and burning.

She groaned. Unable to hold back the incredible need she had for him, the elemental, raw instinct that was driving every caution, every reason from her head.

Suddenly he moved fast, rising above her and pressing onto her body, and she shuddered under his magnificent weight. Mouth open and hungry, she pulled him closer as she let her hips writhe under the wonderfully hard heat of his.

This kiss was utterly erotic—intimate and shamelessly aggressive and she plundered as deeply as he did. She could feel him shaking now too and she swept her hands over him, seeking to touch as much skin as she could. Spreading herself wider beneath his rock-hard body, straining to take him in hand and maximise both their pleasure.

She nipped his wonderfully full top lip. 'Why are you still wearing your shorts?'

He laughed and pressed harder against her, the wet fabric delightfully stimulating against the soft skin of her inner thighs. 'Because I don't want this over too soon.'

'Haven't we waited long enough?'

But his weight had gone and his hands gripped hers, holding them to her sides as he knelt over her, kissing his way from one breast to another, teasing her painfully tight nipples with his hot mouth and wickedly sexy tongue. And then that tongue went lower, circling her belly button and its decorative silver ring and then lower still. He lifted a hand and slid that south too, delving fingers into her curve, parting her so he could kiss that most secret, sensitive part of her.

He gripped her hips now, stilling her writhing

enough so he could extract more from her—more tension, more longing, more need.

But the need to touch him rose, too. She lifted her shoulders from the ground, reaching for him and yanking his shorts down. He groaned as he sprang free and she took advantage of his momentary stillness to move—to explore.

She stroked his silken, rigid length with her fingers and heard him swear. She kissed him and felt him shudder. Then he twisted in her hold, moving so he could touch her as intimately as she was him.

He matched his strokes to hers and she revelled in the freedom of giving her hunger free rein. She breathed in the scent of him, licked the salty taste of him, pressed the hardness of him beneath his smooth skin. She savoured the tension she felt rolling off him. Yes, she could torment him too and she relished it. Her actions grew bolder still, more aggressive, faster, frantic—she was desperate for the pleasures of the flesh and for the white-hot orgasm she knew was almost hers. But suddenly he was gone. Half a metre away from her.

'Ana.'

She whimpered, body trembling with loss. 'Why have you stopped?'

'Because I want more than this.' He tore the packet, sheathed himself with fast, jerky movements.

What more did he want? Mutual pleasure, physical fulfilment— what more was there?

'I want it all.' He rose above her, aligning his length to hers as he looked into her eyes. He laced their fingers together and she could feel him there, thick and heavy against her. So close.

Yes, there was more. There was intimacy, there was that baring not just of body, but of soul. That sharing of the most inner self—and the vulnerability that came with it. And he was seeking it—his ice-blue eyes on fire and searching deep into hers.

He thrust deep, sure, hard. She closed her eyes, tried to absorb the hit of feeling as they locked together again—but she couldn't. Her breath shuddered from her lungs, catching her cry. And in those few moments he regained his control, but hers ebbed. She'd ached for this for too long.

'Please, oh, please.' Her fingers pulled at him, nails curled into the hard muscles, and her hips lifted, forcing the rhythm she so desperately craved, wanting him to drive into her.

And then he did, thrusting deep again, again, again.

Her hands swept over his broad, slick shoulders, revelling in the bulging muscles, savouring the incredibly hard body riding her, rocking into her with a faster, more powerful rhythm than she'd ever dreamed of. This couldn't be wrong. It had to be right. Nothing had ever felt so right.

It didn't take much; it was never going to take much when she'd been so on edge for him for so long. She panted, more audible, more hysterical until all too soon he caught her mouth with his and contained her scream, adding his own groan to it as they shook, reaching the summit and freefalling through the sensations.

CHAPTER SIX

ANA rose before the sun, slipped on a tee shirt and shorts, not bothering with a bikini underneath—just wanting to escape while he slept. Seconds later she left the banda and went for a walk along the beach, eventually succumbing to the temptation and wading into the warm water. She floated for an age, looking out to the horizon where the sky was lightening, and waited for the sun.

She sensed something, looked over her shoulder and saw him watching from the water's edge. The splashes were gentle as he walked in. His arm curled around her, pulling her back against him before she had any chance of escape—not that she wanted to.

His hands spread wide, smoothing over her wet shirt, and then cupped her breasts. She couldn't help herself, leaned back against him. One hand slipped lower, beneath her waistband to where she was really wet. It was mere moments, the fewest of seconds, but it wasn't over. His mouth was hot on her neck, pressing passionate kisses between the words he whispered again, again. 'One night is not enough.'

Until finally she answered him, acknowledging the

truth of it, and offering the only answer she could. 'The rest of Africa. We can have the rest of Africa.'

'Yes.' He hauled her closer, touched her more deeply, and, as the sun rose, made her come.

A bit over an hour later Ana was enjoying fresh fruit and toast for breakfast, relieved to see Seb disappear with one of the island guys for a while. Instead of feeling any kind of release, she was now tenser, more aware than she'd ever been. It had been amazing. His body was that much leaner, stronger and his patience had filled her with awe. Because after those snatched moments in the sea she'd been begging as the void inside had needed to be filled again and he'd happily obliged. Twice.

But now the others were dotted over the beach—either reading in the shade by the restaurant, or soaking up the sun's rays. She sat in an ancient lounge chair and watched the scene, almost drowsy after the total lack of sleep the night before and yet restless—aching for more. She didn't know how long it was later that he appeared, but he pulled her from the seat and kept hold of her hand. Silently he led her across the sand to the water.

The kayak looked way too small and unstable.

He looked at her expression and laughed. 'I'll paddle.'

For the second time that day saying no to him was beyond her. He held the kayak steady and she sat in the front seat.

'How can you do this in the heat?' She pulled her hat lower on her head and felt him push the boat out. 'You're amazingly fit, Sebastian.'

'Why, thanks.'

'No, I mean really. Abnormally fit.'

He laughed. 'I've been working on it.'

Carefully she twisted her head to watch him. 'You really did stop hanging out in the city?'

'I was the epitome of the faithful husband.'

She gave him a long look. 'Are you honestly trying to tell me you've been celibate this whole time?'

'It's not something I'd joke about, Ana. Not ever.'

No sex for the best part of a year?

'But what have you been doing with yourself?' she spluttered. 'I mean…come on, Seb.'

'It wasn't that difficult really.' He pushed the paddle faster through the water. 'I did sport. Multi-sport events.'

'As in triathlons?'

'Yes, something to wear me out.' He nodded. 'Something to focus on outside of work.'

Well, it sure explained the heightened definition his body had.

She sat still and quiet, listening to the water, looking back at the golden sand and the brilliant blue sky. Eventually she relaxed enough to let her fingers trail in the water, watching the island spread wide before her, until she couldn't contain her rapture a moment longer. 'It's incredibly beautiful, isn't it?'

'Yes, it is.'

She glanced at him. 'You're not even looking.'

'Yes, I am.'

Right at her.

She rolled her eyes. OK, so the out-for-fun Seb was back in full force. 'You'd say anything to get a leg over, wouldn't you, Seb?'

'Why don't you believe you're beautiful?'

Because she wasn't. And she'd had years of her aunt emphasising the point. She didn't fit in with the family's perfect, petite, feminine form. She was the prune in the peanut jar. She was going to roll her eyes again but suddenly realised how far away from Zanzibar they'd gone. 'You'd better turn back, Seb. I don't care how fit you think you are, I don't want to be adrift in the ocean for days.'

'We're not going back,' he said. 'We're going there.'

'What?' She turned and saw how close they were to another, much smaller island.

Seb's words were wicked. 'You didn't think I was going to spend another night on the ground or squashed up on one of those hard bunks, did you?'

She sat up so quick the kayak rocked. 'But our packs—'

'Are being transported by another boat. They're probably there already. We came the slow, scenic route.'

'You're unbelievable.'

'Oh, admit it, secretly you're thrilled.'

She looked at the beach they were about to wash up on. Oh, yes. Not even secretly. 'What is this place?'

'This is Mnemba, an exclusive little island. We have our own luxury banda, our own bit of beach and our own butler.'

They had their own butler? That was crazy—what was the guy going to do all day? Besides her Africa trip was all but over. 'Seb, we're supposed to go back to Dar tomorrow.'

'I've changed the bookings.'

'What?'

'We have another few days.'

Another few days? Oh, no. Another night she could cope with, but not more. 'But I didn't even get to say goodbye to the others on tour.'

'They know my plan—at least, Bundy did. He'll have told the others.'

'But I have to catch my flight back to the UK.'

'Give me the details and I'll get it changed. We'll fly back together.'

She hesitated. That wouldn't be a good idea. But then she looked across the water to the beaming man waiting for them, evidently their butler, and beyond to the buildings dotted in the trees. As if anyone could say no to this?

Hamim, their butler, greeted them with true finesse and a wide smile. He offered his hand to Ana as she splashed through the shallows and led her straight to their private apartment. 'You are a model?'

'No.' She shook her head and laughed.

'We get a lot of models stay here. And you have the height, you are as beautiful—if not more so. So I thought...' His smile was even wider.

Oh, please.

'Actually—' Ana smiled brightly back at him and pointed to Seb '—*he's* the model.'

The butler took that one in his stride, inclined his head and left them to discover their accommodation alone.

Ana turned to face the laughing Seb. 'How much did you pay him?'

Seb held his hands up in innocence. 'Nothing.'

Yeah, right.

'Come on,' he challenged. 'Let's check out the facilities.'

In other words go straight to the bedroom.

The view out over the Indian Ocean was open and stunning, and yet there was complete privacy. The furniture was intricately carved and there was comfort in everything. But her bones melted at the sight of the bed—so wide and big.

But it could barely be halfway to midday. As if Seb cared. He ripped off the beautiful white coverings, leaving just the pure cotton sheet on the bed. He looked at the sheet, looked across at her.

'What do you say, Ana?'

'I say there's still a bit of the pirate in you, Seb.' But she couldn't stop the smile. 'Race you to the water.' She flew out the open door down the small strip of sand and splashed into the water, uncaring about her shorts and tee getting another complete soaking. She heard his laugh and dive and licked her lips. Saltwater Seb was a flavour she adored.

Uncaring of the water streaming from her clothes, she walked back inside, peeled off her wet tee shirt and shorts and rubbed the sand from her feet—refusing to ruin the whiter than white linen on the magnificent bed. The sheets smelled so fresh and the bed was soft but not saggy and so easy to stretch out on. Irresistible. She closed her eyes, spread her arms wide and enjoyed the sensation as the faintest of breezes teased dry her damp skin.

Hands on her ankles pulled, yanking her body down over the smooth sheets so her feet dangled over the edge. She opened her eyes and found his laughing right into hers.

'That's what you're used to, isn't it?' His hands slid higher up her legs, creating instant heat. 'Your feet hanging over the edge of the bed.'

'But they don't have to in this one.'

'No.' He lifted her and put her back in the middle of the bed. Took each limb, one by one and spread them so she lay like a starfish. Mesmerised by the look in his eyes, she let him. He ran a finger under the instep of her foot.

'They're huge.' She arched it.

'If they were any smaller, you'd fall over.'

She laughed. Too true.

'Your feet are perfect. Your legs are perfect. No one could resist the silken feel of your skin and your waist is so tiny, your ribs.' He spread his hand across her. 'You think you're such a giant when, really, you're very fragile.' His fingers traced lower. 'Like this, when did you get this?'

Her scar. His fingers underlined her scar. The pleasure she felt from his appraisal disappeared. She forced down the wave of panic. Could think of only one way to avoid the question. She rose to her knees. 'I'm not fragile.'

He was already naked, already aroused and it took nothing to distract them both. Kissing did it—would always do it, she supposed —the physical chemistry was sublime. And in that moment every last one of her reservations fled. This was nothing but a fantasy fling and she refused to let the past reality destroy the moment. She would indulge, have what she wanted—and all of it—on this magical island. She stretched out, so hot, and gloried in his sexual demand.

As he took possession she let her head and shoulders fall, leaning over the edge of the bed, her long hair hanging loose all the way to the floor. She let her arms fall too, feeling as if she were flying as he pounded into her. She curled her legs hard round his waist, and he anchored her core to the bed as the rest of her swung freely through the hot air. She was drenched in sweat— her lower body literally riveted to his and yet she felt so free.

'Incredible.' He groaned. 'You're so bloody incredible.'

Afterwards he grabbed her hand and pulled her all the way back onto the bed. Breathless, she felt insane with the bliss. He walked to the table, sliced some pineapple from the assortment of fresh fruit arranged on a platter. He held a piece to her mouth for her to taste. The juice was deliciously both sweet and acidic. She took the last of it into her mouth. He started to lick the juice from his fingers, but she grabbed his hand, and licked them for him—felt the kick inside again. She had let go of everything now, allowing nothing in her head but the desire—the animal need to be with him. All sensuality, no thought.

His eyes didn't leave hers as, keeping hold of his hand, she lay back on the pillows and demanded, 'Do it again.'

'With pleasure.'

'Maximum pleasure.' She closed her eyes.

Seb looked out the wide open door frame and watched her sitting cross-legged on the sand combing her hair. As beautiful as a siren tempting a sailor to his death. He wished he were combing her hair. He wished she were sitting astride his lap and he were sinking deep into her, and having that glorious hair trail across his face and those long legs wound round him.

She was an incredible lover. Hell, yes, she was incredible. He'd never felt so wanted, or felt such want for another in his life, had been surprised by her hunger and her aggression. Ana was assertive? Why, yes, she was now. If only he'd realised, he'd have come after her sooner.

Every fantasy he acted on he wanted an immediate repeat. And more ideas filled his brain, tantalising him. So now the siren called and he was helpless to resist. He walked out to the beach, took the comb from her hand and did what he'd been dreaming of.

The afternoon stretched long and lazy. He got a bao game and with Hamim's help they learned how to play it. Her competitiveness came to the fore, especially when he proposed an adults-only kind of prize for the winner. He was intrigued by the way her mind worked, the way she skilfully strategised—and he wanted to know more. 'You play chess?'

'Yes.'

'Who with?'

'I used to play with Phil. And then at university—' She broke off and coloured.

'What?'

'My ex-boyfriend thought he could play.'

'You whipped him every time, huh?' Because she was good, she was smart and there was much more to her than big blue eyes and intoxicating long legs.

She nodded. 'He didn't like it.'

'What happened to ex-boyfriend?'

Her eyes dropped to the board. 'He found someone else. Someone shorter. Someone blonde.'

So she'd been cheated on, huh? No wonder she didn't believe him when he said he'd been single all this time. And there was that height thing again. 'Someone crap at chess?'

She laughed. 'I don't know. Probably.'

'That man was clearly an imbecile. When playing for this kind of reward it's not a bad thing to lose to you.'

She looked at him slyly. 'I thought you always played to win.'

'Well, you have to admit this is a win-win situation.'

She dropped some kete into one of the grooves on the board. 'What was it like winning the Robertson case?'

'You know about that?'

'It was in every national newspaper for weeks. Of course I know about it.'

The Robertson case had been ugly. The guy had let his TV talent show instant stardom go to his head. Had ditched his young wife of three years and their newborn babe and embraced the life of the rock star—and the starlet he'd met at the recording studio. He'd thought his newfound money and fame would swing it. Had appointed one of the biggest name divorce lawyers in the city—arguing his new wealth was his and not for sharing with his wife and child. His wife had appointed Seb. At the time it had been the biggest case of his career and had cemented his reputation. 'Robertson had wanted his fight in court. He'd got it.'

'And you won.'

'There were no winners, not in a case like that,' Seb still felt the anger. 'There was a kid, Ana. A kid who when old enough will look back at that case and see that his father didn't want him, didn't want to know him, didn't want to spend time with him and that he was forced by the court to pay money to help raise him. How's that going to make him feel? And it happens all the time. Either the kids are rejected or they're torn apart as the bargaining chip between two bitter parents.'

He always encouraged counselling, mediation, out-of-court settlements—anything to try to make it easier because those people had to deal with each other when they had kids. There was no end, no finality. All it was was a mess.

'Was that what it was like for you, when your parents broke up?'

He froze. Should have known that was where she was headed. That was why he never usually discussed his parents with women—they always wanted to probe deeper than he liked to go. 'I was the bargaining chip, I guess. They both fought for me, over me.'

But even though they'd both wanted him, he hadn't been enough. Not enough to hold them together, not enough to make either of them happy. Most of their problems had been because they hadn't been able to have another child. He—their one child—hadn't fulfilled them.

'I guess being fought over is better than being unwanted.' He glanced up in time to catch her quick flinch and wanted to cut out his tongue. He reached across and touched her hand. 'Hey, I'm sorry.'

'It's OK.' But her fingers slipped from his. 'You're right.'

He'd had no idea about her past. But now he did,

it just reinforced his decision on what he planned to do with his own life. 'I'm never having children.'

'Me, either.'

His brows lifted—didn't all women have a clucky side somewhere? 'Why not?'

She was staring at the board. 'Because I don't want anyone else going through what I went through.'

OK, so they had more in common than he'd ever thought. 'Nor do I.'

She suddenly broke into a big smile. 'Time to pay up, big-shot. I just won.'

The longer they spent playing in the shade, the more outrageous the prizes for winning became—playful, teasing, and at one point, at her instigation, downright kinky. Seb's sense of reality receded. It was like that mad week again—where all that mattered was touching her, being close to her. He simply couldn't get enough.

Ana was brushing her hair when she heard Seb swear. She turned, surprised at the vehemence. 'What's wrong?'

'We're out of condoms.' He growled, a bitter, frustrated sound. 'Hell, the last time we had a holiday fling we got married. This time it'd be just the thing if I knocked you up.'

Her mind blanked. She heard a clatter and blindly reached out; her hand struck the wall. But the pain didn't bring the world back.

'Ana?' He was beside her, his hands on her waist steadying her. 'Are you OK? What happened?'

She opened her mouth to say 'nothing'. But he was so close, watching so closely. She saw as his thoughts tracked back over what he'd said, and down that horrible thorny path. She swayed again, suddenly remembering. It happened sometimes—with something so simple, a word, an image perhaps, just something that triggered the avalanche of hurt. It swamped her. So fresh, so raw, it could have been yesterday.

'Ana?' His eyes narrowed. 'What's going on?' He inhaled sharply. 'No.' He shook his head slowly. 'No.'

She stared, unable to move as she watched him work it out.

'Oh, my God. I did knock you up.' He gaped. 'Is that where you've been this last year—having my baby? Where the hell is it? What have you done?'

'Nothing!' She snapped. 'I've done nothing. You're wrong.' She backed away from him right up against the wall. 'You're so far wrong.'

'No, I'm not.' He followed, trapping her with his big body. 'Don't even think about lying to me. Were you pregnant?'

She closed her eyes. 'Yes.'

'Then where—?' He broke off. Took a breath and spoke with furious deliberation. 'You said you don't want kids. Did you… did you get rid of my baby?'

'Of course I didn't!' she yelled in his face. 'It's because of what happened that I don't want kids. I'm not going through that again. I'm not losing another child again.'

'What happened?' Horrified, he asked, 'Damn it, tell me what happened.'

'I had a miscarriage.' She felt sick as the pain seared into her. She hadn't spoken of it in months but all of a sudden it was present—right in the room—the agony.

'My baby.' His lips barely moved.

'Yes.'

'Miscarried.' He looked down. There was a long silence.

She put her fingers to her forehead. Waiting, knowing the questions were coming and unable to bear having to answer them. She'd never wanted to have to answer them.

'Why didn't you tell me you were pregnant?'

She closed her eyes—just for a moment. 'I didn't want to.'

She heard his sharp inhalation and spoke quickly, preventing his interruption. 'I was hurt.' He'd shattered her illusions so ruthlessly that day when he'd come home more over the moon about his promotion than he'd ever been about marrying her. They'd rowed and she'd run. A couple of weeks later when she'd found out she was pregnant she had still been so hurt that there had been no way she was ever going to tell him. But a couple of weeks after that, reality had started to sink in. 'I knew I was going to have to talk to you. I was just…'

'Just what?'

She sighed. 'Summoning courage.' But then she'd had to find more courage deep inside than she'd ever dreamed she'd need.

He drew another breath, forced it out again. 'Please tell me what happened.'

She was silent. She hadn't ever wanted to talk about it—not with him, or anyone. What was the point? It had happened. It was over. There was nothing he could do. Or that anyone could do.

But her heart sank, for she knew there was no

getting out of it—not with him so close like this, so intensely scrutinising her. He was watching her every blink, her every breath, monitoring her tiny quivering. At the very least she had to tell him the basics.

'I was in Bath—that's where I'd gone after I left you. Everything was OK for a few weeks. I was getting my head around it. Then…' She shrugged, not wanting to go into any more detail.

'Had you been sick? Did you fall?'

'Nothing like that. It just happened. The doctor said I'd never know why. I didn't have any of the usual risk factors. It was just one of those things.'

'But you were going to keep it.'

'Yes.'

His eyes bored into her. 'Would you ever have told me I had a child? Would you ever have found that courage, Ana?'

'Eventually,' she muttered. When she had herself sorted.

'You never should have run away.' He swore. 'Where does it get you, Ana? How can you think you can get away with avoiding everything? Especially something as big as this?' He stood silent for a long time. All of a sudden his body bunched again and he lanced her with an even more intent look. 'Even now you're not telling me the whole story, are you?'

She couldn't hold his gaze, looked to the floor, wanting to disappear into it.

'The scar. My God. This is how you got that scar.' His hands cupped her face, tilting it up to his with surprising gentleness. 'Isn't it?'

Why hold any of it back now? He knew enough, was guessing the rest.

'I had a lot of pain. I fainted. I don't know what happened. I was in and out of it. I remember parts of the ambulance ride. Telling them...' She'd wanted them to save her baby. 'It was an ectopic pregnancy. I went straight into Theatre. When I woke up it was all over.' They'd had to remove her fallopian tube and her ovary had been damaged. She'd stayed in hospital for a few days. And gone back to her empty flat to recuperate—to nothing.

She could feel the tension in his fingers.

'That can be life-threatening.'

Her heart contracted. 'My baby died.'

'You could have too.'

Yes. It had been that serious. And there had been a moment—the darkest of moments—when she'd wished she had. She had lost everything. And had no one and no place she felt she could turn to.

There was a long silence. He didn't let go of her. She could feel his breathing, deep and unnaturally regular as if he was concentrating hard to control it. She waited for the explosion. She could feel his anger like a living thing radiating from him. But it wasn't harsh words and a raised voice that assaulted her senses.

'It must have been awful for you.'

It was a whisper that arrowed straight under her armour. Sympathy wasn't what she'd been expecting.

'You must have felt so alone.' His finger stroked down her cheek. 'You didn't tell anyone, did you?'

She released a shaky breath. 'There wasn't anyone... around.'

There was a moment again, where she felt the wave of effort it took him to stay silent and she could read the hurt in his eyes. She appreciated it. She appreciated it so much that her control began to slip.

'I'm sorry you were alone,' he said quietly. 'I wish you had told me but I kind of understand why you didn't. I just wish I could have done something.'

'There was nothing anyone could do.' Her voice cracked. 'It doesn't matter.'

'It does.' His arms slid around her, pulled her away from the wall and cradled her in a loose embrace. 'It does matter.'

And now, months later—surely too late—he comforted her. And she needed it. How she needed it.

'It matters so much,' he muttered into her hair.

It had. It still did. And she didn't know when the pain would diminish. She had tried to put it from her mind, tried to focus on getting her life back on track and firing up her career. And it had worked—until she'd seen him again. In that instant feeling had started to flow again. Starting with desire at its most basic, but the sexual spark had warmed up all of her emotions. And now that the gates had been unlocked the flood was impossible to stop. Her heart opened and the hurt poured out. His arms tightened, supporting her as she crumpled.

The tears were hot and salty and hurt her eyes and they wouldn't stop. And she couldn't breathe properly, couldn't stop the sobs, the choking as the agony burned its way out. She cried for the things that she'd longed for—for love, for family. And she cried because she simply couldn't keep holding it in. All the while he held her tight, murmuring somethings, nothings, the soft sounds of comfort.

And for once she shared the burden.

CHAPTER SEVEN

SEB watched Ana sleep. He should be running—far and fast. But he couldn't. Just couldn't. He had an inkling of what she must have suffered—and with such quiet strength. Hadn't he seen his mother suffer—for years—as the other children she'd longed for had never eventuated? Hadn't he felt the helplessness, the hopelessness—hadn't he seen the heartbreak?

Yes, he knew something of the devastation Ana must have felt. And even though that baby had been unplanned, even if she'd never wanted children, he could understand why and how its loss had devastated her.

Because wasn't there a hurt inside himself right now? As if a part of his heart had been skinned. A facet of it he hadn't felt before. Hadn't he missed out on something precious too? What would that child have looked like? Would it have had her vivid blue eyes or his pale ones? Undoubtedly it would have been tall and dark…

He closed his eyes and blanked his mind. Not going there. Kids had never been part of his plan—never would be. He inhaled. What had happened was just fate, wasn't it? It was just the way it was meant to be. But how he wanted to make it all go away.

He sat in the chair across from the bed and saw when she stirred. Finally she opened her eyes. From the distance he saw her lose colour as consciousness returned and memory came with it.

She sat up quickly, pulled the sheet up to cover herself. 'I'm sorry I wailed all over you last night. I'm over it. Really.'

In some ways she was—physically over it, and she'd been making plans to get on with her life. That was why she'd sent the divorce papers, wasn't it? She wanted closure so she could move on.

'It's OK. I'm glad I finally know,' he muttered, his voice rusty. 'I'm sorry.'

And he was. Desperately so. But there was still a problem. Closure was elusive—and would remain so unless they worked it all through.

'You'll want to get back to the mainland.' She rubbed her forehead with her fingers, hiding her eyes from him.

'No. I'm not ready to leave the island yet.' He wasn't ready to leave her. For he wanted closure too, wasn't that why he'd come all this way? When, having finally found out where she was, he hadn't been able to just sign it all away without seeing her for himself.

And once he'd seen her, he'd known why he couldn't just sign. It was still there. Just as it was for her. That damn electricity, the inferno that blazed between them. They had to go on and finish it. They'd got off the bus too early last time—they had to get to the end of the ride now.

He tossed the packet of condoms on the bed. 'I got those from the office.' He held his breath. God, could he be more blunt? But he didn't know how else to approach it.

She looked at them and the colour returned to her cheeks in a flood. 'I don't want sympathy sex.'

He gritted his teeth as he heard her anger. 'That's not what I'm offering.' This wasn't bloody sympathy sex. This was I-can't-control-my-lust-for-you passion—and he was desperate to get rid of it. For both their sakes.

'Well, what are you offering?'

'What do you want?' He couldn't stop the rasp in his voice. He knew what he wanted—he wanted as he'd never wanted before. He wanted to make her feel good. He wanted to make himself feel good. Because right now he felt like crap and instinct screamed at him that the only way to feel better was to get close.

She drew her knees up to her chest. Her hair hung in a mess around her face and her red-rimmed eyes were vivid blue and shielded. 'I want what we agreed,' she said fiercely. 'The fling we should have stuck to a year ago. A few days of indulgence to burn it out. Then you go your way, I go mine.'

She had changed. Was tougher—not the marsh-mallow of a year ago. Now she was asserting her desire—and desire was it. He let go his breath with a kind of relief. For wasn't that it for him too? Wasn't that all he wanted—or had he changed?

He stood, unable to keep from moving a moment longer. He couldn't think any more. Couldn't do any-thing but bow to instinct. He knelt on the bed, leaned over her, pressing her back against the pillows so she was in no doubt of his need.

And her hands lifted, fingers wide as she put her palms to his scalp and pulled him closer still. Her mouth opened beneath his and she kissed him with the same sort of desperation he was drowning in.

And for a moment, just a moment, he was sorry she hadn't asked for more.

This was it, wasn't it—the searing attraction, the need for that deep indulgence? Despite everything it was still at the centre of it all. Nothing less, nothing more.

Ana's breath took for ever to regulate, and only moments after it had, she shifted in his arms, woke him, roused him again. Determined this time, to get it right and see it to the end. Because at the back of her mind the clock was ticking—Africa was all they had. When they said goodbye to the heat, they said goodbye to each other.

And she knew she had the strength to do that. This past year had shown her she had the strength to handle anything—even him.

She was glad he knew. Had never thought she'd feel that, but his sensitivity had surprised her. She'd appreciated the comfort of his arms as she'd cried. And she'd seen the hurt in him too—somehow that had helped soothe her own. She wasn't alone in her sadness for the baby any more—he felt it; he understood something of it. And that was enough to make it that little bit more bearable.

They spent the day swimming, sleeping. Not talking of anything but commonplaces, playing bao, keeping it light. And yet they turned to each other even more frequently than before. The passion fast, hungry and still never enough.

The tiny island was exquisite and offered every comfort, yet with the luxury came other facilities—phone, fax, email. In the late afternoon she watched him take his PDA over to the office. Yes. Real life was going to have to intrude—they couldn't avoid the future for ever. She went to their banda, giving him the space to get his messages in private. She didn't want to know, didn't want to become involved in his life back in London. The separation was looming and it was best to start distancing now. But when he walked in twenty minutes later his expression was too grim for her to ignore. 'Bad news?'

He pressed a button and tossed the gadget onto the table by the bed. 'Dad reckons he's getting married again.'

'No way. Who to?' Ana gaped.

'What with Mum going for the fourth last year, they're just a joke.' He flopped back on the bed and pressed the heels of his hands into his eyes. 'I can't believe it. And it's happening Saturday. This *Saturday*.' He groaned. 'So soon—why the hell is he in such a rush?'

The giggle just bubbled from her. 'Like father, like son, I guess.'

'What?' He lifted his head up and then grinned—sort of. 'Oh, yeah. But that's not–'

'Yeah.' Not real. She watched him clearly struggle with the news. 'Does it really matter, Seb?'

'I can understand them having lovers—fine,' he said, throwing his arms wide on the bed. 'Have as many as they want. But what's with all the weddings?'

'You don't think it's kind of romantic?'

'No. It's desperate.'

'Seb—'

'Look, you haven't been ring-bearer too many times over.' He sat up. 'It's tacky.'

'So it's all frills and fifty bridesmaids?'

'Ugh,' he groaned again, but eventually it turned into a laugh. 'Depends. No two are ever the same.'

'Have you met this bride?'

'Briefly.' He shook his head. 'I didn't think it was serious. But I guess he was one behind Mum on the wedding count so he had to catchup.'

'You're kidding.'

'No. Allocation of assets, experiences—they've got to make sure they have exactly the same.'

'But there was only one of you. How did they go about sharing you?'

He looked at her, shrugged in a helpless, resigned kind of way. And instead of answering, he asked, 'Ana…?'

She knew what he wanted. And she gave it.

When she woke late the next morning she found he was already dressed and looking distant.

'You'd better pack your bag, Ana. We're leaving at lunchtime.'

So that explained why he'd barely let her rest through the night. Why he'd woken her time and time again with his incredible caresses. The hour had chimed.

Mentally, he'd already left, his mind miles away as he stared out over the water—clearly not seeing the beauty of it, judging by the size of the frown on his face. Was his problem still his father? She didn't ask; Africa was at an end and she needed to withdraw, too—to handle it with maturity. It was the contract they'd agreed.

Ten minutes later she stood on the deck and watched him swimming, tireless strong strokes as he went back and forth parallel to the beach. She was fascinated.

And then she cursed her idiocy. She wasn't going to stand all morning staring at him. So she went to the main complex, quite determined to find something to do to fill in the few hours till they left. She found the perfect distraction in the beauty spa.

'Where have you been?' He looked grumpy as she strode to where he waited by the boat, the bags already stowed.

'I went for a massage.'

'I'd have given you one.'

She shook her head and laughed. 'You know we're over that.'

He met her gaze for a moment and then looked away. She stood on the boat, smiled and waved to Hamim and then turned her back to the island. Determined to look ahead—in everything.

Only hours later Seb led the way onto the big plane. Ana had never flown first class before and looked around at the amazing space.

'We could have gone another class up.' He watched her investigate all the things in the toiletry bag.

'There's another class?'

'Beyond first class we could have had our own suite.' He looked wistful. 'Big bed and everything. But it was booked.'

Thank goodness for that. She'd already mentally resigned herself to the fact she'd slept with him for the last time. And after what she'd let the beautician on Mnemba do this morning, there was no way she wanted him to see her even partially naked. It had been a good method of restraint.

He read her expression with grim humour. 'You don't want to join the mile-high club with me?'

'Not today.' It wasn't even a lie. Then she saw his surprise turn to determination. Felt his shift towards her as the atmosphere between them thickened to intimate. 'No, Seb, we've left Africa.'

'We're still in its airspace, aren't we?'

'No.' They were over it and she was not, *not*, succumbing again.

Their luggage was the first on the carousel—one of the perks of spending ridiculous amounts of money on seats that became surprisingly comfortable beds. Not that he'd slept a wink of the flight. She pre-empted his move to take her bag, swinging it nonchalantly onto a trolley. He felt super grumpy now.

She turned to him 'Thanks—'

'I've ordered a cab.' He cut her off. 'It should be there by now.'

'Um… I'll be OK—'

'For heaven's sake, Ana, at least let me see you safely to your place.'

They walked to the rank and he climbed into the cab after her. 'You're staying with Phil?' he asked shortly.

'Yes.'

A flare of jealousy spiked into Seb's chest. Stupid. He wasn't surprised Phil hadn't said she'd been staying with him. His loyalty was greater to Ana than to him. But it annoyed him nonetheless. If Phil had been honest he might have got to Ana before she'd gone to Africa. Hell, how long had she been staying there?

Added to that, the thought of those two guys sitting either side of her on the sofa drinking their soy decaff lattes or whatever namby-pampy juice was flavour of the month, listening to her pour heart and soul out to them, got his hackles on end. She'd talk to them as she didn't to him. God, had Phil known about the baby—his baby?

The cab pulled in front of Phil's building. It wasn't far from Seb's home. But it was far enough to bother him. 'I'll help you with your bag.'

She raised a single brow. It was only the one pack but he was delaying the inevitable.

She rang the bell. 'I have a key if they're not home.'

Of course she did. But they were home. The footsteps came faster; Seb glared up at the security camera.

'Ana!'

It was Jack—Phil's partner. The most conservative-as-they-come accountant you'd ever meet in your life. Older than Phil by a good ten years, he was the anchor to the flamboyant interior-design genius who'd just appeared in the doorway behind him.

'Darling.' Phil pushed past Jack and hauled Ana into his arms. 'I was beginning to think you'd been eaten by a crocodile.'

'Something like that.' Ana's tone was caustic.

'Seb.' Phil's eyes glinted as he tilted his head to see who was behind her. 'The crocodile, I presume,' he added, closing the door behind them.

Ana turned, looked surprised to see Seb still standing there. 'What about the cab?'

'It can wait. The meter's still running.' He wasn't ready to leave yet.

'Drink, Seb?'

'Thanks.' He followed them through to the lounge. He'd had no intention of stopping for a drink. A quick goodbye and that was it. But perversity seemed necessary right now.

Phil sent him an assessing glance and went straight to the harder stuff. 'Whisky?'

'Thanks.' Single malt. One thing to be said about Phil, he had impeccable taste.

'I might just put my bag in my room.' So Ana wanted to run, huh?

'Jack will do it, darling,' Phil said smoothly. He took a sip from his glass and then smiled. 'Fancy you two meeting up in Africa.'

'Just fancy,' Seb said coolly, refusing to rise to Phil's stirring. Ana would find out it had been her friend who'd told him where she'd gone. What she would read into that he was sure he didn't care.

'I didn't know you guys knew each other all that well.' Ana hadn't touched her wine. She looked tired and suddenly Seb's arms ached with emptiness.

'Seb's a client now,' Phil answered.

'A very valuable one,' Seb added drily. He'd paid a huge fee to Phil. But he'd been worth it. Purely for the fringe benefits—namely his association with Ana. Phil had all the info. But even he hadn't revealed she was actually staying with him.

Seb felt anger ripple through his body. He was angry about having to leave her here. And even angrier about feeling angry about it. He should be relieved. He should be over it. He'd had more sex in the last few days than he'd had all year. And the best sex of his life, if he stopped to think about it. Which he didn't want to do, because now it was over. He stood. Time to go.

Phil and Jack were unusually silent, unusually observant as Seb waited for Ana to walk out to the hallway ahead of him.

She opened the front door and waited. He looked at her but she looked through him. All the intimacy was gone. She didn't lean towards him, didn't smile, just stood stiffer than a starched collar. It really was over for her, wasn't it? She couldn't wait for him to leave.

So he didn't kiss her. Held back with more muscle control than he needed in the last leg of a triathlon. Angry with everything. Because it was what they'd agreed—Africa and that was it. Cut and dried, and damned if he was going to mess it up any more.

But the sharp edge of loneliness dug deep in the drive to his apartment. Cold, he tossed his bag by the door. He'd deal with it tomorrow. Better still get his laundry service to deal with it. He switched on his stereo to try to block the silence. Felt wrong inside. As if his stomach and his lungs had swapped places or something devastatingly uncomfortable.

Jet lag. That'd be it. Tiredness from the long flight. There was work to get on with and plenty of it, he noted as he skimmed his emails. There were details from his Dad as well on the next wedding of the century. Hell, if he had to work on another divorce for either of his folks that was it, he was charging them full fees. He shut down the computer, turned off the stereo too and cranked up the heating. He passed his bag in the hall, bent and pulled out the wooden bao set he'd bought on a whim on that last day. He held it in his hands, remembered the hours of frisky entertainment the game had spawned. Irritated, he put it high on the overcrowded bookcase and turned his back on it.

It. Was. Over.

CHAPTER EIGHT

'SPILL it, Ana.' Phil was sitting next to Jack on the sofa and together they were acting like an incompetent good-cop-bad-cop interview team.

'Phil, she'll talk if she wants to.'

'I'm her oldest and dearest friend. I have the right to know.'

'Only what she—'

'I don't need all the details, just—'

'*When* she's ready to tell you.'

'Why don't you go do the dishes? She'll open up to me.'

'Maybe she'd rather speak to someone who actually *has* ears, not ones that are just painted on.'

Ana watched them digging at each other with the teasing glint so evident in their eyes. Their banter was never serious and always cute. But tonight it grated. 'Can I say something?'

'Sure.' They simultaneously turned their heads towards her with synchronised Abba-esque speed.

'I'm going to get an early night.' She stood.

'Oh, yeah, you must be worn out from all those hot

nights in Africa,' Phil said, more sarcastic than sympathetic.

'The flight was long.' She aimed to quell.

'And cosy. Bet you went business class.'

'First class. It was very spacious, actually.' Liar. She'd been too close to him for her nerves. Now they were beyond frayed and almost at break point.

'Come on, Ana. The guy follows you halfway round the world. You can't have *nothing* to say.'

'Look,' Ana said tiredly. 'It *was* nothing.'

Phil pounced. 'So there was an "it"? Define the "it".'

'Why do you want to know?'

'Because I'm worried about you!' He walked and put his hands on her shoulders. 'You looked washed out.'

'I told you the flight was long.'

'It's more than the flight.'

'Well, what little there was is finished now.' Ana sidestepped and moved to the door. 'Sorry, Phil, but I really am tired.'

'But—'

'Leave it,' Jack said to Phil.

But Phil didn't leave it. 'I thought you'd come home happier than this.'

'What do you mean?' She looked at him.

'I thought…' He frowned. 'Ana, there's so obviously something between you and Seb.'

'Something. Yes. We slept together again, Phil— is that what you wanted to know?'

'So now what?' He looked confused.

'Now nothing.' She shrugged, not wanting to feel confusion herself. 'It's over.'

But Phil frowned, followed her to the door. 'Last time you hooked up with him you went away together for a week and when you got back you then disappeared for *months*. Now you've had another week or so away with him—can you blame me for wondering what is going to happen next?'

'Nothing's going to happen, Phil. We've just... scratched the itch. Finished off the unfinished business,' she said, unable to find a better cliché.

'Can women do that?'

'What?'

'Well, you know, be so casual? I always thought it was harder for you to take the emotion out of sex.'

'It's hard for anyone to divorce emotion from the act of love,' Jack chimed in.

'Oh, please.' Ana rolled her eyes. 'It wasn't an act of love. It was lust. Pleasure. Physical need. Nothing more.'

Phil and Jack stared. Silent. Sceptical.

Ana sighed. 'Goodnight, guys.' She strode to her room, focusing on one thing only: sleep—blankness of mind, *nothing*.

During the day she got busy with work. Went window-shopping. Immersed herself in the smells and sounds and sights of the big city—filling her senses with so much stuff that thoughts of the beach, the sand, the silence and the sex were banished from her mind.

But at night she tossed and turned and told herself again and again that the itch was all gone.

Friday she walked into the kitchen where Phil and Jack were opening a bottle of wine for their post-work snifter. 'Let's go out to dinner. My treat.'

'Yeah?' They looked delighted.

'Yeah.' She held up a pair of shoes she'd once

thought she'd never wear. 'But if you see me talking to a tall, dark, handsome stranger, come and smack some sense into me, OK?'

'Deal.' Phil laughed.

Ana grinned. 'I need to get out.'

'Yeah, you need to show off that tan.'

Seb knew the minute she arrived. Of course he'd had his eyes glued to the door so it wasn't as if she was going to be able to sneak in without him knowing.

Even so his body seemed to sense it was her the second before she stepped into the bar. Adrenalin zinged along every vein. And unerringly she saw him too—in that first instant. Her brows lifted, something flashed in her eyes but he didn't have the chance to read it—too soon she'd veiled them, too soon she'd looked away.

But she sidestepped her way through the other patrons and came over to him. Smile in place. 'I didn't expect to see you here. I thought you said you'd forsaken this kind of lifestyle. Aren't you all about mountain biking and marathons now?'

He eyed her over the rim of his glass. 'And I thought you'd be too busy setting up the business to have time to socialise.'

'No. I can do social as well. I feel quite refreshed after Africa.'

She looked it too, damn her. Whereas he felt like death warmed up. Hadn't slept properly since he'd got back. Cold. Lonely. Grumpy.

'I'm getting the drinks.' She looked at his half-empty one. 'You need another?'

He shook his head. Phil took her place as she moved over to the bar to order.

Seb glanced at him. 'Thanks for your message.'

Phil didn't smile. 'Make no mistake, Seb. I'm Ana's friend.'

Seb smiled faintly. Was this Phil attempting some sort of overprotective attitude towards Ana? The guy didn't know it but she was totally capable of taking care of herself. 'So am I.' Sort of. They had some kind of connection that counted, didn't they?

He'd been going to come here anyway—whether he'd had the message or not he knew full well it was Phil and Jack's favourite haunt and that if they were going to take her anywhere, it'd be here. He'd just wanted to see her. Now he had.

'Are you going to join us for dinner?' Phil asked. 'We're just waiting on a table at the Thai place across the road.'

Seb couldn't stop staring after Ana. 'I'm not sure it's such a good idea.'

'Thought you said you were friends. I'm sure Ana won't mind.'

Yeah. That was what he was afraid of. That she didn't care enough to mind. But he couldn't resist staying, could he? 'OK.'

Fairy Godfather Phil—that was what he wanted to be. Ana glared at her friend. It was better than having to spend any more time looking across the table at Seb. Because seeing him made something twist inside her. For once it wasn't his gorgeousness heating her belly. If anything he looked less than his usual immaculate male-model self. He looked tired around the eyes, maybe even thinner. And it was that causing the discomfort inside her.

She abandoned her dinner. Noticed he'd stopped eating too. She couldn't resist prying just a little. 'You're not with your dad tonight?'

'He's not having a stag do if that's what you mean.'

'What time is the wedding?'

He shrugged, his brow wrinkling. She wanted to smooth it. His eyes, in just that second, looked so unhappy. Sure he was laughing with Phil and Jack, sure he was making the effort. But that was what she sensed—the effort it was taking him. Clearly the whole wedding thing was cutting him up. The ridiculous urge to comfort him flooded her—she wanted to hold him and make him laugh. Make him carefree again.

Careless.

Where had the fun-loving Seb gone?

As the evening progressed the urge to reach out to him only grew. She'd thought she could handle it. She really had. At last they headed back to Phil and Jack's—running the few streets in the drizzle. Phil and Jack took the mickey about her shoes and Seb's smile flashed in the dark as she ran faster than all of them just to prove herself.

The guys insisted Seb stop for another drink before going on to his apartment. Phil opened his whisky and the three parked in the lounge. Ana tried to join in—fixed herself a hot chocolate and acted as if none of it were a problem. But in the end all she could do was run away.

She lay in bed and listened to the deep voices. The laughter resonated up the wooden stairs. But in her mind's eye she saw him with that pain in his expression. It had been a mere flash but she knew it went deep. She sighed. What was she doing *caring*?

She finally slept—waking to hear Jack remonstrating with Phil, telling him to hurry up. She glanced at her watch—after ten already. The boys were off to Manchester for a couple of days to see Jack's family and they had a long drive ahead of them.

She pulled on jeans and a tee. Wandered down and grinned at Phil's greenish tinge and dark glasses. 'Late night?'

'Early morning,' he grumbled.

She walked him to the door. Jack was wrestling with an oversize suitcase, trying to jam it, and the other twenty bags, into the boot of his car, muttering about the amount of stuff Phil insisted on taking with him.

Phil sighed. 'He loves my high-maintenance tendencies, really.'

'Of course he does.' Phil was exceptionally high maintenance but he was also such fun. 'Have a great time.'

Phil turned back and took her wrist. Usually his face was lit with laughter but now he was serious. 'Don't run away again.'

She hadn't contacted him during the time she'd hidden away down south. He hadn't told her off, had never pried—not about that. Just opened his door, taken one look and let her in. So she owed him now and gave a promise she was determined to keep. 'I won't.'

The sparkle in his eye rekindled—sly this time. 'Are you going to go wake Sleeping Beauty?'

'I suppose,' she said darkly.

'Don't do anything I wouldn't.'

Well, that gave her a hell of a lot of leeway, didn't

it? He winked and she waved. She walked back into the apartment and glanced at the immobile log still sound asleep on the sofa, then at the empty bottles on the table. Clearly a very early morning for them all.

In the kitchen she got the espresso machine working. Made it so strong it was like thick brown goo dripping into the cup. She lifted the cup and wandered back through to the lounge. Held the steaming brew under his nose.

'Wake up, Seb.'

One eye opened and quickly shut again. 'I'm dreaming.'

'No, you're not.'

He peered at her again. 'Ugh. You're right. If I was, you'd be naked.'

'Sebastian, you have to get up. Aren't you due at your father's wedding?'

'Not going.' His growl took her aback.

'What?'

He sighed. 'Look, I have no interest in seeing my dad get married again. Certainly not to a woman only a few years older than me.'

'Seb.' She shook her head. 'Aren't you the best man?'

'Been there, done that. Twice already. Not gonna again.'

'Seb, this is your father.' He couldn't skip this. He'd regret it. She knew he would.

'So? I don't know her family. There's not a lot of mine. It's not going to be fun, Ana, and it'll all be over in a year or two at best. What's the point?'

'It's not about having fun. It's about being there for your family.' She paused.

'Not going.' He lifted his head from the sofa and raised his voice too. 'They're too annoying.'

'You should be grateful you have parents to be annoyed by.'

His head thudded back on the cushion. 'Oh, you had to go low, didn't you?'

'Yeah. You can't argue with me.' She handed him the mug. 'Drink up. I'll take you back to yours and drive you to the wedding.'

'I'm perfectly capable of driving.'

Like hell he was. 'With the amount you obviously drank last night? So much you couldn't walk the three blocks back to your place? It's still got to be in your system.'

'I didn't have that much. Not enough anyway.'

'Well, you smell like you're over the limit.'

Seb grunted. Unable to deny his amusement. Yeah, he reeked. But that was because in the carousing with Phil he'd spilt a giant glass of Scotland's finest over his clothes. Terrible waste. But it had got late and Phil had been keen to stay up later—sly dog. He'd known, hadn't he, that the last thing Seb had wanted to do was leave? He'd tossed him a blanket, telling him it was too cold/wet/late to walk home—making it easy for him. And Seb had practically leapt at the offer. Hell, he'd slept better on this too small sofa than he had in his own right-sized bed. Just knowing she was near. That he was going to see her again soon—in only a few hours rather than the uncertain number of days he'd had to wait this week.

Hell. There was something seriously wrong with him.

'I'll walk home.' He needed to get his head together.

'I'm coming with you.'

His mood inexplicably lifted. 'Why?'

'Because I have the feeling you're not going to show up at the wedding. And I think that would be a mistake.'

He eyed her lazily. He didn't give a damn about the wedding. 'What are you going to do about it?'

'I'm going to take you there myself.'

'You're inviting yourself to my father's wedding?' His heart stopped beating.

'Yeah.' She tossed her head. 'Why not?'

Why not? Hell, she had no idea how close he was to giving in to base urges and hauling her into his arms. His heart thumped again—a couple of uneven beats before picking up speed as his brain processed the idea of having the whole day with her. 'You want to see what the craziness is like?'

'Is it that crazy, Seb?'

'It's hell.' He closed his eyes again as he thought of something far more wickedly exciting. 'What are you going to wear?'

There was a bit of a pause. Then he heard her soft voice—heard the catch of shy laughter.

'Actually I have the most amazing dress. A few, in fact. Want to help me choose?'

'OK.' Of course he did.

'I'll go get them.'

'*No* to anything black,' he called after her.

In a minute she was back, holding a hanger with a dress floating from it. 'No black limits options. What about this?'

He stared, his whole body reacting, and was damn glad of the blanket he still had over him. 'Have you ever worn it in public?'

'No.'

He almost managed a laugh.

'What do you think?'

Her eyes were wide, her teeth caught on her lower lip. He thought he was about to burst out of his skin with lust.

He forced his eyes back to the dress. It was green or maybe blue, a shimmering slip of a thing with spaghetti straps. And short. Far, far too short.

'You can't wear that.' That was what he thought.

'Why not?'

'Because it looks like it belongs in a bedroom.'

'You think?' She grinned. 'The woman in the boutique assured me it was for evening wear.'

He bet she had.

'It has a wrap that goes with it. So I won't freeze.' She was looking at the dress again thoughtfully. 'But I can't wear a bra under it — the straps will show.'

'Wear strapless.' He choked.

'I don't have strapless.' She frowned and then smiled. 'But I can get one. We can call in at Harvey Nicks on the way.' She shook the dress on the hanger so it shimmered more. 'And I can't wear knickers—the lines will show.'

Oh, she just had to be doing it deliberately. 'Umm.'

'G-string.'

'OK,' he said roughly. 'Sounds good.'

'So you'll go, then?'

What choice did he have? 'Yeah.'

Ana barely suppressed her giggles as she walked with him to his apartment. The look on his face had been priceless. No bra? No knickers? Ana had never had the experience of turning someone to jelly at her feet before. It was hilarious—and heady. But he had to go to the wedding. If she had to hog-tie him and carry him in there, he had to go. She knew what it was like to fall out with family. He was hurting now—if he didn't show he'd hurt more. He had parents who loved him—who'd made life hard, for sure, but who had loved him. Where there was love there was hope, right?

She looked around his apartment as he disappeared upstairs. It was totally different from when she'd been in there a year ago. It had been stripped and modernised. Light and spacious, the kitchen was fantastic.

'What do you think?' Seb called.

'Phil did a good job.'

'Yeah.' He walked through to where she was with just a towel slung low round his hips.

Ana stared. He'd shaved. He'd showered. He'd gone back to gorgeous.

'What are you doing?' she asked, unable to tear her eyes from his frame.

He hadn't dried himself properly. Droplets of water clung to his chest —tracking down his oh-so-toned abs. Her body began its meltdown—Seb and water. There was nothing like Seb and water.

He looked surprised at her question. 'Need to iron a shirt.'

Not sexy. Not sexy. Seeing a man in a towel ironing a shirt was not sexy.

Right—her boobs weren't getting the message. Nor was her womb.

Ana had to put herself in time out. 'I'm going to get to grips with your car.'

She took his key and went out to where the sleek

machine was parked. Tossed the bag with her shoes and dress into the back and sat in the seat and figured out the windscreen wipers.

He grinned wickedly when he slung into the seat beside her. 'Harvey Nicks, here we come.'

Ana kept her eyes on the road. She hadn't seen Seb in a suit in a while. And if she looked now they'd have an accident. Fatal.

But Seb had come to life. Any trace of hangover was obliterated as, frighteningly at ease in the lingerie department, he happily browsed through the racks of silk and lace and nothing-much-else. He held up a couple and looked surprised when she turned on him crossly.

'Can't you go and be embarrassed in the corner like any normal man would?'

'And miss out on all this? No way.' He grinned as her colour rose. 'All right, I'll go look at the bikinis. That make you happy?'

Ten minutes later she stood in the booth and sighed. There was no denying it. There was no bra on earth that could be worn under the dress. She had to go commando.

'You can get away with it. Not many could.'

Oh, hell, she was going to have to walk in public like this? Thank heavens for the wrap. Ana turned to the assistant. 'I feel bad about not buying…'

'Don't worry. Your husband is out there buying up a storm.'

'He is?' *Her husband*? He'd announced their relationship to the store?

The woman nodded. 'Now he's sure of your size…' Her brow raised.

Ana didn't need the mirror to know she was cherry red. The shop assistant clearly thought there was some kind of Pygmalion thing going on with her and Seb because she'd already sent for one of the girls from an exclusive make-up counter.

'It won't take a moment to touch up your face.'

Touch it up?

'This is all part of the service?'

The assistant smiled. 'We like to take care of our valued customers.'

Goodness. He really must be spending up big.

She sat on the chair in the spacious changing room and held still for the 'touch up'. Glancing into the mirror, she couldn't believe the effects wrought after just a few dabs here and there. And the lipstick was just the shade.

'You'll want one to refresh later.'

'Sure I will,' Ana said. 'Just add it to his bill.'

They bonded more over her high-heeled strappy sandals.

'Some time today would be good.' Seb's voice came through the curtain.

'Ignore him,' Ana said sotto voce to the assistant. 'I do.'

It was another full ten minutes to get finished and then summon the confidence to exit the room. She couldn't bear to wait for his reaction so went straight on the offensive.

'What are you buying?' She stared suspiciously at the tissue-wrapped somethings going into the big bag. There was already one full bag to the side of the counter.

'Nothing.' Evil grin in place. 'Wedding present.'

'You're giving your father's new wife frilly knickers?'

She moved closer to see them, still not looking at him, noticing instead how his hand had curled into a fist on the counter.

'What did you do to your arm?' The laugh in his voice had vanished.

'Oh, nothing.' Damn, he'd seen it through the wrap.

'Nothing doesn't need a plaster.'

It was the thinnest plaster she'd been able to find. But it was a big square—had to be, to cover her moment of lunacy. 'All right.' She breathed out and prayed for cool indifference. 'I got a tattoo.'

'What?' He pushed the shawl back, his fingers gently lifting the edges of the tape. 'When?'

'On Mnemba.'

His fingers stopped. '*Mnemba*? I didn't realise there was a Tattoo You on the island.'

'Oh, yes. They had everything there. I got it on the last day when I went for that massage and you were swimming.'

'A tattoo. Needles, Ana? In Africa?' Now his fingers were gripping her too hard.

She rolled her eyes. 'It's henna, Seb. It'll fade.'

Colour slashed his upper cheeks and she felt his harsh breath out. 'So why are you covering it up, then?' His fingers were back at work, carefully peeling the sticky tape.

She held back the wince and made her excuse. 'It's not exactly classy, is it, for your dad's wedding?'

'Dad's wedding isn't classy.'

He lifted off the plaster. Damn. She instinctively rubbed her arm, hoped by some miracle it would have faded in the last sixty minutes. But from the impenetrable mask that his face had just become, she knew she'd had no such luck.

They were a regular sideshow for the shop assistants, weren't they? Discreet as those perfectly coiffed women were, they weren't able to hide either their smiles or their interest. There was a long moment of silence during which all the indoor plants decorating the room grew an additional three inches from the heat radiating from her face.

Finally he spoke. 'What does it stand for?'

'South Africa.'

Their initials were entwined in the centre of some completely intricate swirling, flowery design that was in a sort of oval shape covering almost all of her upper arm.

'You seem to have been misinformed— We weren't in South Africa. We were in Tanzania.'

'The girl did it,' Ana mumbled—mortified. 'It was her idea. The design.' Oh, hell, this was too embarrassing. 'They thought we were on our honeymoon.'

'I told them we were,' he said so softly she hardly heard. She was too busy trying to explain.

'She'd done it before I knew. I… I thought it was just going to be a…a pretty pattern…' Her feeble mutterings ceased as she felt his finger trace over the letters, following the swirls down her arm.

She looked at him; his smile had disappeared altogether.

'I'll put the bandage back on.'

'Leave it.'

'I have the wrap—it'll cover it. It's cold anyway. This dress is too short.'

'The dress is stunning.'

She didn't listen. Too busy staring where he was rubbing his hand over his jaw. 'You'd better take your wedding band off. Why do you wear it?'

'Because I'm Mr Married at work. Why didn't you take yours off?'

'I did. Months ago.'

'Rubbish.' He picked up her hand. 'The tan mark is still there. I saw it days ago.'

'I only had it on because the travel guides suggested it for women travelling alone.' She snatched her fingers from his.

He made a sound that suspiciously sounded like a snort.

She glared at him. Forgot the assistants. Forgot everything but how close he was now. And he glared back. Then—as if he couldn't help it—his gaze coasted down her body. She felt it like a caress.

He shook his head the tiniest fraction. 'Your shoes are ridiculous.'

'Too tall?' There was only an inch between them now—both in height and distance. She could almost look him in the eye.

His arm snaked round her back, pulling her in tight. 'No.'

She was flush against him. Could feel him. Oh-h-h, could she feel him.

'Just about right.' His mouth so nearly brushed hers.

But just as abruptly he turned and walked, pulling her quickly out of the store.

Ordinarily Ana would accuse someone moving this fast of being flustered. But Seb never got flustered. People stared as they moved through the departments.

But then, they always stared at her. It was just a fact of life when you were taller than most men. But in this dress, these shoes and, yes, the lipstick, she felt a million dollars—all because of the passion she'd just seen in his eyes.

He wanted her. Badly.

So let them stare—she no longer cared.

OK, so maybe most of the stares from the women were aimed at him. And the smiles definitely were. He guided her through the store, gripping the thousand bags in his other hand. She was breathless. Totally turned on high. Definitely wanted to explore the hitherto unrealised potential of the shoes. Stand-up sex—they hadn't done that on Mnemba. Amazing when she considered they'd done it just about every other way. A wave of pure eroticism trammelled through her. Fiercely she celebrated the freedom that came with the flush of that heat. She could be her own woman—in charge of her own body, her career, her assets and most of all her heart. She could handle *him*.

She got into the car. Strapped in and checked the mirrors, pulled into the line of traffic and relished the power beneath her fingers and feet.

She could feel Seb's eyes on her, could see the sexy half-smile on his lips and the way he was turned towards her.

She glanced across to meet his eyes. 'What?'

Despite his shave he still had an air of dissipation about him. And he spoke with the sort of sultry, hours-spent-in-bed tone that made her bones melt. 'You suit being in the driver's seat.'

CHAPTER NINE

ANA pulled up outside the venue—one of those all-in-one wedding venues. An ex-palace or something with beautiful gardens and old stone walls. She let the car idle.

'Out you get. I'll be back in three or so hours.'

Seb stared at her.

She smiled. 'You didn't really think I was going to crash your dad's wedding, did you?'

He didn't smile back. 'If you don't go in. I don't go in.' Utterly uncompromising.

'Seb, this is for your father. This is just one of those things you have to do.'

'You in or I don't go.'

'I can't. I'm not invited.'

His expression didn't alter. 'I'm inviting you.'

'Seb, I can't go in. I can't wear this.' She inhaled—he didn't get it, did he? 'For heaven's sake, Seb, *I'm not wearing a bra.*'

He threw his head back and laughed. 'Oh, honey, I know.' He laughed some more. 'What's the problem? You didn't wear a bra once in Africa.'

'That was different. I wore a bikini.'

'Well, you just walked through one of the busiest stores in London in that outfit and everyone stared because you look so damn hot. Now get out of the car and let's get this over with.'

Ana's heart thudded. So damn hot? She felt it. When he looked at her like that she felt it. But this was awful. This was just awful. She'd only dressed up to prod him into going. She'd had no intention of actually going through with it.

He was looking her over, very thoroughly, from head to toe. 'If you don't get out of the car now, I can't be held responsible for my actions.'

Sweating. It was a mid-winter, miserable London day and she was dissolving into a warm puddle. Ana pulled the key from the ignition and gave it to him to pocket. 'We're not in Africa now, Seb. Let's go.'

Out of the car she positioned the wrap around her shoulders—aiming to cover both breasts and the tattoo. He waited on the footpath for her, then walked with his hand at her back as they went in. It was a far bigger do than she'd anticipated and she was ridiculously glad of her 'touched up' face and heels and designer dress. Even more glad of the wrap. People smiled at Sebastian, looked interestedly at her when he introduced her as his 'friend'.

'Darling!'

'My mother,' he muttered in her ear, quickly informing her as the woman rushed forward to greet them.

His *mother* was here? Wasn't that awkward?

'I haven't seen you in months. What have you been doing? You've lost weight.' She looked at Ana as if it were all her fault.

'Mother, this is Ana. Ana, this is my mother, Lily.'

Ana smiled, pulled the shawl that little bit tighter around her arms. So this was her mother-in-law, huh? Good grief. This was total madness. But Sebastian had a twinkle in his eye and she just knew he was enjoying her awkwardness.

'Sebastian, you're doing the business for your father.' Lily turned to her son.

'Again,' Seb drawled.

Ana gave him a look. 'Don't spoil it.'

His brows lifted and their gazes clashed. 'I won't.'

'So, Ana,' his mother said firmly, 'you can come and sit next to me.'

Like a royal summons, the demand couldn't be ignored. Ana sent Seb a terror look, which he countered with a grin that said she deserved it. She pulled her wrap closer around her so she didn't give the woman an up-close view of her tattoo.

But in moments she forgot the discomfort as the ceremony got under way. It wasn't tacky, the bride— who was definitely more than a couple of years older than Seb — did wear white, but it was a suit not a lace and sparkle-encrusted meringue. Their vows were simple, and their smiles were huge. Ana thought it was sweet.

And then she looked at the tall, dark-suited man standing beside his father. He was staring at her. And he wasn't smiling. And as soon as the formal part was over he walked over to her.

'They look really happy,' she said, wishing he could find some joy in the occasion.

'For a limited time only.'

'You are so cynical.'

'Why will this one last when the others didn't? Second, third time round are even less likely to go the distance than first-timers.'

'But some do, Seb.' His stubborn disbelief annoyed her. 'You're so determined to think the worst, to expect the worst. It surprises me that a person as competitive as you should be so defeatist.'

He looked startled for a second but quickly covered it.

Well, if he wasn't going to enjoy himself, she was. She nobbled a passing waiter and took a glass of champagne.

Seb finally smiled. 'Taking advantage of the free booze?'

'Isn't that what weddings are for?' Besides, she could do with a little Dutch courage.

'Too right.' He lifted a glass of juice from the waiter's tray and winced. 'Except I can't face it.'

He couldn't face the whole thing, could he? Heaven forbid these people actually made a *commitment*.

'Good. You'll be OK to drive and I can kick up my heels.'

'Fantastic—you can warm up and lose the wrap.'

'You're not afraid I'll make a spectacle of myself and embarrass you?' some internal imp made her ask.

His gaze travelled over her slip of a dress. 'I'm half hoping you will.'

Ana withstood the heat for a moment. They were flirting with danger again, weren't they? But it was worth it to see him smile.

She turned away from him in time to see Seb's mother embrace first her ex-husband and then the latest of her replacements. 'I thought you said they were really bitter.'

'They are. They just hide it under a layer of superficial niceness.' He looked at her sardonically. 'For my benefit, of course. They wouldn't want to openly fight in front of the boy.'

'Are they that bad? Or is just you who's so uncomfortable with the situation?'

'What do you mean?'

'Look, Seb, I don't blame you for being bitter. I don't blame you for feeling hurt. But why won't you give them a chance? You just refuse to believe in them, don't you?'

'There is no such thing as for ever, Ana,' Seb said shortly. 'Not ever. They've proved it enough times already and I don't know why they bother continuing to try.'

Ana turned, unable to look at the harshness in his usually so handsome face, and stared at the fairy creature who'd appeared right in front of them.

She had blonde hair. Natural too, the cow, with bright blue eyes and make-you-blink white teeth shown to complete advantage in a wide, pretty smile.

Ana blinked, refocused and then tried not to stare with complete jealousy at the woman's petite figure. She had the slightest shoulders, her tiny collarbones set off by a beautiful necklace that Ana just knew was a one-off collector's piece. And she was short—slight enough for any man to scoop her into his arms with ease. So feminine. So lovely. So everything that Ana wasn't.

'Sebastian!' The elf threw her slender arms around Seb's neck. 'So nice to see you!'

Ana saw his hands go around her waist. Figured she was so tiny he could probably touch his fingers and thumbs together in a complete circle. And in that low-cut top and slinky skirt? She had the 'gorgeous slim socialite' look down pat—was a complete, genuine beauty.

Ana felt the clumsy, gawky, overgrown teen inside her tear off her superficial layer of mature, confident adult. Suddenly she was sure that if she tried to take so much as a step she'd probably trip over, or bang into the corner of a table. That if she tried to talk it'd be some squeak of stupidity. That her feet were bigger than Ronald McDonald's.

This girl was a flawless diamond, and Ana was an oversized lump of coal.

She didn't even look at Ana. At least, not initially—not while she was busy leaning into him with the brilliant smile in place, utterly Miss Effervescent. Then she turned her head, still pressing into Seb, and subjected Ana to a totally different sort of smile. The sort that was still vivacious but that held none of the flirtation and all of the challenge. Oh, yes, the petite piranha had her teeth in and she wasn't letting go.

'Ana, this is Cassie. Cassie, Ana.'

Ana was surprised he could still speak given the way the woman had invaded every inch of his airspace.

'Ana? How lovely to meet you!'

Oh, could she be more sparkly? Ana felt snark in every cell but she managed an almost smile and waited for her to let go of Seb.

She soon realised she was going to be waiting a long, long time.

'It's been too long, darling!' Cassie was patting his chest—stroking, in fact. 'You've been working too hard. You obviously need to have some more fun.'

There was a flashing look beneath her lashes at Ana then—a flash of a knife. 'When are we hitting the club scene again? Later tonight?'

And Seb, damn him, was smiling right back, his lazy charming smile, and he wasn't stepping away from her full-frontal contact.

'Not tonight, Cass. This wedding is enough excitement for one day.'

Ana watched the pout of disappointment and then the resurgence of that brilliant smile as Cassie tried to secure his company for another night. Was she an octopus? She had hands everywhere.

'I'm sorry.' Seb shook his head. 'Will you excuse me? I have to go grimace for some photos.' Seb finally put his hands on Cassie's and removed them from where they seemed to be smoothing over his entire torso.

Photo call, huh? Ana was jealous—of that and a lot of other things right now. He'd better not be planning on leaving her with this predator.

'You two have a lot in common.' Seb actually managed to tear his gaze from the lovely blonde one and look at Ana. 'Cassie loves accessories.'

Yeah, of the tall, dark and handsome variety. And he really was leaving her—walking off with a look of total, possibly evil, amusement. Ana stared after him, tossing an imaginary dagger or two into his back. Then she turned to face the ultimate in competition. She might as well roll over and surrender now.

'Have you known Sebastian a while?' The petite piranha was quick to skewer her with the smile and the questions.

'Yes,' Ana said carefully. 'A little while.'

'We go way back. We're very close.'

Ana just bet they were. 'How lovely.'

There was a moment when they smiled insincerely at each other.

'You've a fabulous tan for this time of year,' Cassie then commented. 'Gosh, I just couldn't go in the sun like that. I wouldn't want to damage my skin.'

'No? Shame.' Ana smiled sweetly. 'We've just got back from Africa.' *And it had been so worth the skin damage, darling*, she added under her breath.

'Africa?' Cassie's sharp eyes narrowed. '*With Sebastian*?'

'Yes.' Desperate to put this woman in her place, she couldn't resist recklessly adding, 'It was our honeymoon.'

'*Your honeymoon*?'

For one second, absolute triumph zapped through Ana. Unfortunately it was instantly zapped by a regret so awful she felt sick. She wanted to retract. Immediately she drained her glass and escaped to the bathroom. But when she walked out five minutes later she saw blondie in earnest conversation with Sebastian's mother.

Oh, no.

She met the ice-cool gaze of his mother with a flush, helplessly watched as the older woman turned and went to Seb, interrupting the photo call as she asked the question.

By rights the glass windows should all have shattered. The decibel of the shriek certainly had all heads turning.

'You're married.' His mother's voice carried clearer than a bell.

Seb, standing to the right of his father, turned and looked across at Ana. She lifted her head, meeting his eyes full on and determined to hold onto her justification. She had some somewhere—didn't she?

And all of a sudden she was trapped between him and his mother, who was firing questions machine-gun style.

'When?'

Seb looked at her. Forcing her to answer.

'A while ago.'

'Where?'

'A registry office.'

'A registry office? Oh, Sebastian.' His mother looked appalled. 'Let me guess, no witnesses, no guests, no party. You've never had the celebration.' She tutted. 'Never had the first dance.'

'It wasn't something that interested either of us,' Ana muttered.

'Sebastian, how could you?'

'Quite easily.' He finally spoke. Cooler than Arctic waters. 'I figured you and Dad have had enough weddings between you. You didn't need me to add another to the calendar.'

Ana looked at the expression in his mother's eyes and for the first time realised that their mess of a marriage might actually hurt someone other than herself. This was the woman's son—her only child—and she was finding out about his wife for the first time at her ex-husband's latest wedding. It must be a bit of a shock.

'Will you excuse me a moment?' Another bathroom trip was definitely in order. To give them a moment. To escape from the energy she could feel in Seb—the *angry* energy.

Mistake. Big, big mistake.

He was waiting for her when she emerged and she didn't have the courage to look at him.

'I thought we were going to keep the details under wraps,' he said a little too quietly.

Ana knew the colour in her cheeks was delirium-fever red—and only deepening. 'Well, Cassie was digging her elbows into me as she tried to plaster her breasts all over you.'

His lips were firmly pressed together. Too firmly. After a silence that stretched Ana's nerves to utter defence mode he finally spoke again. Still soft, still dangerous. 'You're not jealous, are you, Ana?'

The woman was blonde and petite and beautiful. Of *course* she was jealous. Not just jealous but threatened, insecure and apparently capable of a lioness-like display of alpha-girl territorial behaviour. Since when did she do that? And yet her claws itched to be unsheathed again just at the thought of the woman. Not that Ana wanted to admit to any of it. 'I…er…'

'I've never been interested in Cassie,' Seb said evenly. 'She's the daughter of my father's friend. I've known her most of my life and I've never even kissed her.'

'Although I'm sure you've had the opportunity.' Ana just had to dig.

'Sure. But I didn't take them.'

Them? As in more than one opportunity? So the vixen had been hunting him for a while, had she? Ana's claws sharpened enough to cut more efficiently than a diamond-tipped blade.

Seb stepped closer. Took hold of her chin in firm fingers and made her look at him. To her surprise it was amusement glowing in the depths of his eyes, not anger. And while his voice was still low, it was threaded with a half-laugh that made her spine go scarily soft.

'If I wanted to I would have a long time ago. I didn't want to then, don't want to now, won't ever want to. Satisfied?'

The guilt was sloshing around inside with an unusually large dose of embarrassment. But there was a warm twist of pleasure too—and, yes, *satisfaction*. Then the embarrassment gained supremacy. 'I'm sorry,' she mumbled. 'I'll leave. I can just sneak away.'

'No, you can't,' he said calmly. 'You have to smile your way through this as I do. It's your fault for announcing our marriage so smoothly. You were the one who insisted we come. I'd have skipped it altogether.'

'*I* didn't want to come. I just wanted *you* to.'

He shook his head and pulled her wrap from her shoulders, baring her arm, and her body in the silk dress.

'What are you doing?' She reached for it but he tossed it onto the nearest chair—grabbed her by the arm to stop her following it.

'I think the least you can do is give me something good to look at.'

'Seb.'

His smile was wicked. 'Ana, what you and I need to do is make the best of a bad situation.'

Somehow she got through the dinner. The jokes. The speeches. Smiling hard, she watched the cake being cut. Finally it was the first dance. A few songs after that she was sure they'd then be able to leave. Ana watched the couple walk to the middle of the floor. Heard Seb groan as the musicians struck a few chords.

'It's a snowball,' he muttered.

'Snowball?'

Seb shot her a pained look. 'Not up with wedding traditions, are you?'

Ana watched, mystified, as the couple began to waltz. She couldn't see the problem; they looked sweet. And then the musicians seemed to pause—holding the note. The bride left her husband's arms and went and got Seb. While his father went and got her bridesmaid—then another chorus of the waltz was played and the two new couples danced. Another pause. Seb went to his mother and the others found new partners. They waltzed round the room for another chorus. Then came the pause again. And Seb walked to her.

She got what he meant now—the dance was repeated over and over, with each pause those dancing would go and get a new partner. Snowballing—slowly expanding the participants until all the guests would be on the floor.

She stared at his outstretched hand. 'I don't want to dance, Seb.'

He pulled her into his arms as if he hadn't heard. The music began and they moved around the room. Finally, thankfully, the pause came. But Seb didn't move. Didn't let her go.

'Aren't you supposed to get another partner?'

He shrugged. 'I like the one I've got.'

'Even though I keep standing on your feet?'

'Just stand and sway.'

And so she did. Turned her face into his neck and breathed in his scent, unable to meet his eyes for long. The expression in them was too overwhelming.

* * *

She was like a sea goddess. The pencil-slim shimmering dress deepened her blue eyes, her long glossy hair hung loose, and with her skin gently golden from the sun and the deeper brown henna tattoo across it she looked stunning. She was so lovely he nearly swallowed his tongue. It felt as if it had grown to three times its usual size—but it wasn't only his tongue getting thick.

His heart beat uncomfortably hard as he realised just how much he'd wanted to hold her again. And now that he was, he was in no hurry to let go.

He watched her; with the shoes she was wearing she was only a little shorter than him and he could see almost levelly into her eyes. Or he would be able to if she actually looked at him. And suddenly it struck him—that was the thing, wasn't it? For all the fantastic sex they'd had, she never looked him in the eyes— at least not for long. She took pleasure from him, burned under his touch, but refused to connect with that simplest of intimacies.

No more.

'Ana.' He felt an utter compulsion to reach through to her. 'Don't go remote.'

'What?'

'Look at me.'

He knew his mother was watching. And his father. Both were staring over the shoulders of their partners. But he didn't care what they thought. He just wanted to be with her. It was all he seemed to want.

She'd enjoyed the wedding. He'd watched her face during the vows, seen her smile. Could see the way she was glowing now. Yeah. She loved the whole deal. She'd want the big performance one day. And how would she look in a traditional wedding dress? With a veil wisping over her hair and face and the bloom of radiance that he had to admit did descend over a bride?

He pulled her closer. She followed him easily now. Her body soft against his. Then her leg tangled, brushing too close, and his pulse went even more erratic. She was going to be the death of him. He hauled her even closer and gave up on the trying-to-step bit. Stand and sway was all it could be. Her lids had drooped again, but it was different this time. Masculine pleasure filled him for he knew the reason—desire-drugged, she couldn't keep them open.

He let her have a moment and glanced down at her arm. It looked as if someone had drizzled melted chocolate over the caramel skin of her upper arm. He ached to taste it. To run the tip of his tongue over the swirling design. OK, he was glad it wasn't permanent, but it was fun for now. Just like the rest of her—right?

Fun for now. But their fun was over—closure. They were supposed to have left the lust in Africa.

'Ana.'

'Yes?'

'You're not looking at me.'

'I'm looking at your chin.'

'Look into my eyes.'

'You want to hypnotise me or something?'

Part of him wished he could. He had no idea what she wanted from him. Did she want to kiss him the same way he was dying to kiss her? With the same kind of desperation? She wasn't saying. But now he longed to know exactly what she was thinking. Why she was thinking it and what was she feeling for him?

Or maybe he didn't want to know. In case it wasn't the same.

He was losing track of his thoughts. So gave up and just sealed himself to her, lost in the blue of her eyes and the soft invitation of her mouth.

Closure? Who was he kidding?

Ana's head was spinning and she was needy. The kiss was incredible. Soft and gentle and not enough. She wanted more—she wanted it all. But now the waltz was over. She wanted the cheesy music back. She wanted his arms back.

But he stepped away, breaking the contact. Putting on the brakes.

And then his mother was there, all over-bright eagle eyes, and his father too. She managed to be polite but inside she was bursting. It hadn't gone—hell, would it ever go? This desire she felt for him?

And he knew. Played on it—making the best of a bad situation? He did that by invading every inch of her personal space. His hands didn't leave her body—either he held her hand, or rested a palm on the small of her back, or slung his arm along her shoulders, his leg pressed to hers as they chatted to his father's friends. And he looked at her—the *way* he looked at her. As if she were the most beautiful woman on the planet.

He made her feel like an enchantress. And she longed to be able to cast a spell—so she could get herself some kind of fairy tale.

Stupid. She already knew the power to make her life something special was in her own hands—down to her decisions.

So she gave up on the bubbly and switched to mineral water in an attempt to regain sanity. But it didn't help her increasing temperature—the need spiralling through her system. She was hotter than she'd ever been in Africa—and now glad of her skimpy dress. She couldn't be this close to him and not have him.

'Are you ready to leave?' His eyes searched hers.

She looked away from the heat in them. 'Whenever you are.'

He had the goodbyes done and them out of there in under ten minutes.

They drove back through the dark, wet streets. It was late but she wasn't tired. Every sense wide awake.

'Did you have a good time?' He finally broke the silence.

'Yes,' she admitted honestly. 'Did you?'

'Yeah. Parts of it were pretty good.'

He pulled into a parking bay a couple of spaces from Phil's building. She felt a bite of disappointment. There'd been no invitation back to his place. It really was over, wasn't it? He might have flirted, might have stolen a kiss, but when it came to it, he was playing safe.

He turned off the engine and looked at her. 'Thank you for coming with me today,' he said gruffly.

Well, neither of them had *come*. But she wanted to. Badly. Once more the recklessness flowed through her veins—the damn-it-all-to-hell burst of 'I want' that had swept over her in Africa.

And so she moved, undoing her seat belt and leaning towards him. She did what she'd wanted to do all evening. Hooking her hand round his neck, she brought his mouth back to hers.

What caused this madness? Was it the champagne or the frock or the whole shock of the evening when they'd been exposed as almost newly-weds?

None of the above. It was pure Seb. From having him so close and not touching him the way she'd ached to for seven or so hours. The pressure had mounted inside her, now it was on its unstoppable release. And with the rush of sexual adrenalin she remembered there were benefits to simply taking what you wanted. To just going for it. Excitement—raw and intoxicating.

He had long legs and so the driver's seat was positioned back as far as it could go—meaning there was plenty of room between his chest and the steering wheel. She used all of it. Straddling him, her dress slipping up as she spread over him, she unfastened his trousers.

'Ana.' But he didn't resist. Indeed his hands helped, his mouth settling on her most sensitive areas. He knew. He knew so well how to please her.

It was quiet and dark on the London street. But inside the car their breathing was harsh and fast and their movements frantic until the blissful moment when she pushed down so he was deep inside her. She clenched her muscles hard to hold him. Loved the raw groan that shook him.

'I thought we weren't in Africa.' He nipped the side of her neck and she shuddered with delight.

'This is hotter than Africa.'

'Sure is.'

His hands slid over the silk of her dress, seeking skin, seeking to slow. But she rode him fast, catching his mouth to muffle the sounds as they both came too quickly.

Only moments later, panting, she understood the futility as the surge of bliss waned and the hunger returned threefold. This wasn't enough. It wouldn't ever be enough. Chasing fulfilment in this physical way was a mistake.

Damn.

She'd opened his door and was off his lap before Seb could blink, let alone breathe.

He leaned out and grabbed hold of her hand. 'You're not inviting me in?'

'I don't want to disturb Phil and Jack.'

Given that those two were a couple of hundred miles away, he knew that would be impossible. She'd just lied—using them as an excuse to stop him from spending the night with her. Ironic when she'd been the one who'd just ravished him. But now she was running. Again. He let her go. 'OK.'

He watched her fly to the door as if the devil were at her heels. Looked down and saw he still had his seat belt on. He half laughed, figured she'd just put a whole new spin on the concept of safe sex. Yeah, real safe sex. The sort of sex where she didn't look him in the eye and didn't deal with him after—neither physically or emotionally. The sort of sex he'd had most of his life. And while it was frisky and fun, wickedly exciting, all of a sudden it wasn't enough.

Something savage burned deep inside his belly. No. He didn't want sex like that any more. Well, he did, but he wanted even more—he wanted to hold her close in a big bed for *hours*. He wanted her to look at him, laugh with him, damn it.

He inhaled a deep, totally rationalising breath of extremely frosty air. It was just the hit he needed. Hell, what was she doing to him?

'Hey, Ana,' he called as she stepped through the door. 'Who's the pirate now?'

CHAPTER TEN

SEB knocked harder on the door of Phil's apartment, finally heard Ana's thumping footsteps and grumbles as she opened it up. He raised his brows at her appearance. Somehow her tan had got sallower overnight; dark circles ringed her eyes.

'Your hangover's that bad?' He walked straight in.

He'd spent the whole night awake reliving those frantic moments in the car when she'd ravished him. His heart still thundered with the recollection, making the blood surge vitally through his veins. For the first time in days he felt alive. Whereas she looked queasy. That made him nervous.

'Why are you here?'

'Have you eaten?' He ignored her bald question. He'd deal with that once she had some sustenance.

She shook her head, looking pinched at the suggestion. He didn't think she'd had that much to drink at all. 'You should—'

'No, thanks, Seb.'

At the very least she was having a coffee. He went to the kitchen and started fiddling with Phil's espresso machine.

She sank onto the sofa and stared at the black boots on the floor in front of her. 'Why are you here?'

He sat next to her, tapped his finger on his knee and figured he might as well get it over with. 'I don't know if you realise this, Ana, but we didn't use a condom last night.'

To his intense surprise she laughed. 'Oh, don't worry about that.'

Don't worry about it? After what she'd been through?

She shook her head. 'I'm on the Pill, Seb. I'm fanatical about it. Besides, I'm down one tube—there's less chance of a successful pregnancy.'

Oh. OK. The Pill. Good. That was good. She was safe. And he didn't need to feel as if there were needles being rammed in him all sides over.

But he did.

Less chance of a successful pregnancy.

Right.

The silence grew. He watched as she slowly shrank deeper into the sofa. All of a sudden he knew he had to get out—and that he had to get her out. To fresh air and salt water—to where he could clear his head and she could hers. 'Come on, we're going for a drive.'

'I don't want to go for a drive.'

'Tough.'

It wasn't the result of too much alcohol making Ana feel queasy at all. She'd only drunk a couple of glasses of bubbly. But she'd let Seb think it was a hangover— that way she could explain away that hussy moment on drink rather than desperate desire.

She'd thrown herself at him. Literally launched herself aboard and stolen a ride. One that hadn't been enough. And that was what was really making her sick. She still wanted more. One look at him in his jeans and charcoal jersey and she was all warm mush inside and longing for things neither of them wanted. Seb wasn't into for ever and she was building her business —so she could build her life around that. And that was why she had to do this now.

She had to stop seeing Seb.

Today was the day.

Yet somehow she was walking out with him. Feeling her cheeks flush as she slid into his car. He lightened the drive with idle chat, chat and more chat. It was amazing how he could keep a conversation going all by himself.

'Are you still alive?'

OK, so he was clued into her quietness. She smiled. 'I'm enjoying your waffle.'

It wasn't all she enjoyed about him. And that was her problem, wasn't it? It wasn't just the sex that she liked— she liked him all round. And, knowing him the way she did now, she knew that was doubly dangerous for her.

They finally arrived at the seaside. Walked for an age on the sand—not speaking, just stretching legs and listening to the seagulls. Ordinarily such exercise would soothe her. But she was too anxious for it to work today.

'Let's get an ice cream.' He looked so vital—his face full of colour and humour.

'Seb, it's freezing.'

'Ice cream usually is.'

'No, I mean the weather.'

'But we're at the beach and when at the beach—'

'We need to stop this, Seb,' she said quickly.

He stopped talking and walking. Their eyes met.

'Last night—'

'Was a mistake.' She interrupted him again. 'We need to stop.'

She needed to stop.

She turned and walked back towards the car. There was nothing more to say. Nothing more she could say because the side of her head was suddenly pounding as if a hundred tribesmen were beating drums inside it. She needed to close her eyes. She needed to lie down. Why was the car so far away?

'Ana?' Seb's hand clasped round her upper arm as she swayed.

'I'm OK.'

'No, you're—' His curses made her head hurt more.

'Migraine. I've just got a migraine.' The pain intensified in seconds, ratcheting up to unbearable. 'Let's go. I want to go.'

Blindly she turned, screwing up her eyes to block the vicious light. His other arm was at her waist, she felt him guide her, push her into the car and felt him reach across to do up her belt.

'I'm sorry.'

'Don't be silly.' He shut her door. In seconds he was in his seat; the engine purred as he got them away. But the waves of agonising pain worsened. She couldn't get air into her lungs. She breathed harder, faster, but still it wouldn't work. Panicked, she felt the pain in her head pulse with increasing fervour. Her mouth filled with poisonous-tasting spit.

'Seb!' She warned him just in time.

He pulled over and she got the door open and leaned into the gutter. The sickness was violent and hideous.

She groaned, embarrassment adding to her overall vile feeling as she felt his hand rubbing gentle circles over her back. But then the pounding in her head resumed so badly she no longer cared.

'There are wet wipes in my bag,' she muttered. 'A little packet.'

'Wet wipes.' She heard the smile in his voice, then the rustling like grenades detonating in her ears. Then she felt the coolness on her brow.

'I can do that.' She moved too fast and winced.

He pushed her hand away.

'Seb,' she whispered, now mortified.

Gently he turned her head towards him and smoothed the wipe over her forehead and down. She opened her eyes, wanting to apologise, but his expression was too tender for her to bear. She closed her eyes once more.

He reached across and redid her belt. She leant her head against the seat, unable to move at all. Even a fraction caused such throbbing pain.

It felt like for ever that they were driving but finally he switched off the engine. She opened her eyes and looked.

His house. Not Phil's.

'Come on, honey.' He had her door open, scooped her into his arms.

'Seb, you'll break your back.'

'Shut up.'

She did, burrowing her head into his broad chest, too sore to love the fact that she was actually being carried like some feather-light feminine princess. Mercifully soon they were on the second floor and in a big bedroom and then into a room off that. He lowered her onto a chair. She heard his footsteps sound on the tiles, a drawer slide open and then close again.

'Ana.' He handed her a new toothbrush and a travel-sized pack of toothpaste and left her alone. He was always prepared for an overnight guest, huh? But her head already hurt too much for her to add that to it. And honestly she was just so grateful to be able to brush her teeth.

After she'd freshened up she slowly went back into the bedroom. He met her halfway across the floor. Carefully he slipped the shirt over her head, smoothly got rid of her trousers. The covering on the bed was already pulled back and the curtains drawn. The sheets were cool, the room dark. Shivering, she rolled onto her side, burying the blinding side of her head into the pillow. The mattress depressed further. She exhaled as he took the space beside her. But he said nothing, didn't move more other than to put a gentle arm over her hip and cradle her back against him. Slowly his warmth seeped into her. She felt sleep start to claim her. The relief was immense.

When she woke she turned her head experimentally, felt the rush of relief as she realised that the headache had gone. But even better than that, he was curled around her—arms about her, his legs entwined, keeping her warm with skin on skin. He was naked—and hiding nothing, certainly not his hardness.

'Better?' His whisper was sweet in her ear.

'Yes.'

He rolled her to face him. She looked into his all-serious eyes.

'We're not stopping,' he said quietly. 'Not yet.'

She tried to turn away, to slip from the bed, but he stopped her with the weight of his body and a kiss that stole her breath.

'Your migraine yesterday proves it,' he said when he finally lifted his head.

Yesterday? She'd slept through a whole night? 'Proves what?'

'That you're not ready to walk away just yet. That you're stressed about it.'

Of course she was stressed. And that was exactly why it had to stop. But he didn't give her the chance to say it—his mouth caught hers again, silencing them both for long moments.

'Listen to me,' he muttered. 'Look at me.' His hands moved, tormenting with their slow caresses. 'If you don't look at me, I'll stop.'

What choice did she have? Silently she stared up at him.

'You have the most incredible legs. So long, so smooth, and up here—' his fingers caressed the inner part of her thighs '—so soft.'

So what could she do but spread them further?

He smiled. 'And your breasts. Oh, your breasts.' He bent and took a nipple into his mouth—one then the other. 'So perfect.'

He shifted, settling his weight in place, kissing her again as she melted around him. 'And here—' he slid home with a groan '—you have the hottest place a man could ever hope to find.'

She had to close her eyes; the sensation was too overwhelming for her to cope.

But true to his word he stopped moving. And then withdrew.

'No,' she whimpered.

'Look at me, Ana,' he said softly, his hand cupping her chin.

She did. His eyes were piercing and yet tender.

'If you want me, you have to stay with me.' He pressed into her again.

She shuddered, blinked rapidly.

'Right with me,' he warned.

She licked her lips but couldn't look away. It felt too good. He was too good.

Their faces were mere inches apart, and there wasn't a millimetre between the rest of them as their bodies fused. She stared into his beauty, knew that he was seeing right through her. They'd never been so intimate.

'But the most beautiful thing about your body is your eyes. No, don't close them. Let me see.'

And she let him, as slowly, silently their bodies meshed together, parted, and then merged closer still. Her breathing hitched. So did his.

She wanted to beg him not to be so gentle. That this tenderness was too much. But she could say nothing. For her heart was bursting—surely about to break. But then it wasn't breaking. It was expanding—filling with warmth from the look in his eyes. And she could resist it no longer.

He didn't speak again. The palm of his hand cradled the side of her face, stopping her from turning away from the intensity of his gaze. But she couldn't, even if he let her. Those ice-blue eyes of his had melted and inside them she could read all the things she dreamed of yet dared not. That he meant his sweet words, that he wanted her, that he cared.

But she daredn't believe. And the effort not to was pulling her apart, until she was unable to stop the stinging sheen blurring her vision.

He kissed each tear away and his whisper roared loud in her heart. 'But even your eyes aren't as beautiful as your soul, Ana.'

And with every long, slow thrust he tore down the last of her defences.

Overwhelmed, unable to stand it any longer, she reached up for him, captured his beautiful mouth with her own. The kiss went on and their arms wound tighter around each other. She closed her eyes but couldn't keep anything back. Not as she felt his body flex even stronger, the groan reverberating in his broad chest as he began to move even more powerfully. And all she could do was cling, let her body move, her mouth move, touching him, pulling him closer. *Urging* him to finish it.

His fingers tunnelled into her hair, firmly keeping her face turned up to his as he broke the kiss and relentlessly bored into her again.

'Please.' She wanted faster—had to have it that way or she was sure she'd die.

But he resisted, kept it slow, so slow and so deep for so long. She was mindless with desperation, her cries sounding higher and higher. Until with an almost inhuman scream she hit the edge and went hurtling light years beyond her limits.

On and on the climax went—almost brutal in its intensity. Her fingers clawed into his muscles; her body shook with the fierceness of it.

And still it wasn't over, still he moved, still unbearably slowly, overwhelmingly intense. His face darkened, taut with the effort, his body slick with sweat. Until he could hold back no longer, deep groans of male pleasure racking him.

She shook, her arms and legs curled tight—clamping around him. And it felt as if he were pouring everything she'd ever wanted into her.

She refused to open her eyes now—not wanting to break the spell that she was under, the sublime, treasured feeling. But moment by moment reality impinged. He'd moved just slightly, so he wasn't crushing her, and she listened as their breathing returned to normal.

He'd just broken her heart. She knew he hadn't meant to, but he had. No matter his old playboy habits, in his own way he was caring. He'd known she'd felt low and he'd set about making her feel good the best way he knew—with fabulous, sweet sex.

But that was all it was. Short-term charm. Because that was all Seb ever did—flings. Fun affairs. And knowing more of his background now, she even understood a bit of why he wanted only that.

She closed her eyes. The problem was that what they'd just shared hadn't been fun to her. That had been *everything*.

How could she have thought she could handle him again? She was such an idiot. But she wouldn't make the same mistake twice. Wouldn't ask him for more—demand what she knew he had no desire to deliver. Mortification resurged—it had gone bone deep when she'd realised he hadn't married her because he was madly in love with her; she didn't want to be so foolish again now.

What she needed was a little defence. OK, she just needed to get out of there.

'I need to get back to Phil's. He'll be expecting me.'

'I'll call him. You're still tired.'

'I can call him.'

But it seemed Seb had already spoken with Phil at some point, because when Ana spoke to him the plans were already in place.

'I hope you don't mind, darling, but I packed up most of your stuff. I've had a shipment of fabric in and haven't got anywhere else to store it.'

'Of course.'

'You stay with Seb, darling. He has much more space there.'

It was a conspiracy. So much for the gay man being like a sister in solidarity, this was the boys clubbing together.

'You sound tired. You could do with some rest.'

She could hear him smiling as he spoke.

'I've had a migraine.' They'd only had sex the once; it wasn't the all-night orgy that Phil was so clearly imagining.

She pushed the 'end' button on the phone and turned to watch Seb dress for work. 'You set that up, didn't you? With Phil already.'

He shifted so she couldn't see his face. 'I wanted you to stay.'

'Why didn't you just ask me to?'

'Because I thought you'd say no.'

Did he really not know? Had he not worked it out? She was trapped. She didn't want to say no to him. And now, after this morning, she *couldn't* say no to him—not any more.

* * *

Seb gave her a sideways glance as he did up the buttons on his shirt. She was too quiet. And still way too pale. The sudden onset of her migraine yesterday had frightened the hell out of him. He still wasn't breathing right—the tightness in his chest not easing. It was as if he was permanently on alert for some kind of catastrophe—all adrenalin and edge. Not even being so deep inside her this morning had helped. In fact that experience had only seemed to make his sense of urgency worse. He'd said she was stressed about it and maybe she was. But so was he.

She had to stay with him. Despite knowing it meant their affair was growing in complexity, there was no question about her leaving. Not while she looked so ill. And no way was she sleeping in any bed other than his for a while yet.

'I won't be here more than a day or two, Seb. I'll find another place.'

'Just relax, Ana. It doesn't bother me.' Only a bit. He was feeling his way—blindly working on an instinct he hadn't yet identified. 'I'll bring your things back at lunchtime.'

'You don't have to do that. After work is fine.'

That was too many hours away. He needed to check she was OK before then. He walked over to the bed. Exerted formidable restraint and didn't kiss her—knowing he'd never get to work today if he did. But he did touch—a gentle push to make her lie back on the pillows. 'Stay in bed. You need sleep.'

Half an hour later he looked at the files piling high on his desk and shook his head. How many marriages had he helped end now? Must be hundreds. And so easy it was too. A piece of paper here and sworn affidavit there. It was the division of assets that got the game trickier. No one wanted to give anything material up. It was all about protecting their interests. And Seb always did his best for his clients.

Unless there were kids. And then, he'd have to admit to himself, he'd try to do what was right for those kids. Always took stock of the psychologists' reports if there were any. Recommended counselling—did his best to insist on it. Because he'd been that kid—more than once—witnessing the end of another marriage and being pulled in a million directions. Weirdly, as his clients had become wealthier, more famous, the money thing became even more of an issue—the lifestyle to which they were accustomed had to be maintained. Yet there was often more than one ex in the mix. Kids to more than one mother. The mess was horrendous.

At least he and Ana didn't have any such worries. Dissolving their paper marriage would be easy. They had their own assets and they'd invested nothing in the marriage. And there were no children.

His heart seemed to stutter every time he thought of that—the child they'd lost. So he pushed it from his mind by sheer iron will. She said she didn't want kids. Neither did he. And that was a good thing, wasn't it? Because it meant that maybe their affair could continue—maybe indefinitely. OK, there was never a 'for ever', but they could be together for as long as they both wanted. There was no fear of the complication of children. And no real commitment. And given that he desired her more than ever—this could only be a good thing. Even so he should push the divorce through—he could sign those papers today and get the process under way.

But instead he lifted the first file on his desk and opened it. Fee-bringing business first.

An hour later he shut the file—having got nowhere. His mind had drifted further than a piece of cork on an ocean.

He'd go get her bags and take them to her now. So what if lunch was still hours away—she'd need something clean to wear, wouldn't she?

He laughed as he carried the bulky bags straight up to his room and dumped them on the floor. He walked into his big wardrobe and pushed his clothes to one side.

'You take this half.' Although judging by the number of bags still in his car she might need the one in the spare room as well.

She was sitting on the bed wearing his robe and he pounced on a bag spilling shoes to stop himself pouncing on her. She was still too damn pale.

'My God,' he teased as he tipped the bag up. 'You weren't joking about your collection.' At least twenty pairs of sky-high heels had piled out into a mountain.

'They're pretty good, aren't they?'

'Most look unworn.'

'Most are.' She looked sheepish. 'I can't part with them. They're a reminder of my stupidity. And the fact is I still love them. But I've been wearing them more and more.'

'I've noticed.' And he liked it.

He handed her some hangers and she took one bag into the wardrobe, started pulling out her shirts and hanging them up. He set to sorting the shoes—finding the mates and lining them up. He found another bag of them, pulled shoes out one by one and set them in place. Definitely going to need the wardrobe in the other room. He delved deep into the bottom of the bag and found another smaller bag. He opened it and pulled more shoes out. But they weren't high heels. They were sneakers.

Baby-sized sneakers.

His heart didn't just stutter. It stopped.

Quietly he reached into the same bag and found another three pairs of baby shoes. Both genders covered. He laid them on the floor in a row.

'Ana?'

She stepped out from the wardrobe, saw them immediately—*stared* at them.

He stared at her.

'You kept them.' He finally regained the power of speech.

Her lips twisted. 'I keep everything, Seb. As you can see.'

But this was different. 'You said you don't want children.'

'I don't.'

'So why keep them?'

'I didn't keep them. It's just that I never get rid of anything. I'm a hoarder.' She didn't look at him as she answered—walked back into the wardrobe. She might sound casual, but he knew what she was doing— hiding.

Seb felt sick as he stared at the shoes once more. Of course she'd kept them—deliberately. She'd wanted to keep them—safely tucked away in a little bag at the heart of her collection. Just as she'd wanted to keep their baby. She wanted children. And she couldn't—shouldn't—deny it. She shouldn't deny what was true to her. She shouldn't try to be like him. That was what she was doing, wasn't it? She'd learned all the wrong things from him. Like their fling—their deal in Africa—that wasn't in her character. The dreamy-eyed woman he'd met a year ago wasn't the kind to instigate a quick and meaningless affair. She *felt*. She was a soft, loving woman who really was meant for love and family.

Her keeping the shoes revealed that, didn't it? Just as the glow in her face at his father's wedding had hinted that her romanticism, her idealism, still lurked beneath her shiny new carefree surface.

She wanted more. And she deserved more.

But he wasn't the man who could deliver it.

He clenched his fists as an ache ripped through his guts. 'What are you going to do with them?'

Ana pulled her face from where she'd buried it in the clothes she'd just hung in the wardrobe. Inhaled deep to steady her voice. 'I don't know.'

'It's not like you'll be able to rent them out.'

No, of course she couldn't. Anger spurted inside. Why was he pursuing this? What did he want her to say? She marched out of the wardrobe and scooped up the shoes, stuffed them back into their little bag. 'I don't want them.' She tossed the bag into the hall. 'I'll put them in a charity bin later.'

She needed some kind of superglue to fix the tear in her heart—fast—because she didn't want the hurt to burst out again. Not now. Not when things were confusing enough. But it was rising fast—and was huge again, hitting her in a wave.

Damn. Why did he have to find those shoes? And why was he freaking out about them?

'I have to go back in to work,' he said briskly. 'Lots to catch up on still since I was away. I'll be back tonight.'

Yeah, he was backing off fast.

'Of course. I've got work I need to get on with too.' And she needed to shower, dress, get a life. Because if she was reading his expression right, they were pretty much over.

'Use my study.' He didn't touch her as he left.

'Thanks.' She swallowed, unable to believe his coolness—that he could shut down so quickly. Especially after this morning.

Wow.

She pressed her hand to her chest, squeezed out the memory of how he'd held her so tenderly only a couple of hours ago. She couldn't think on that any more. Then she closed the door on that little bag out in the hall.

She'd been right yesterday. It was time to end it. But she wasn't going to run away—not this time. She'd wait and see him, tell him she was pressing ahead with the divorce.

Closure would be hers.

CHAPTER ELEVEN

SEB looked up at the tall figure who'd just cast a long shadow across his desk and drawled, 'Don't tell me you want a divorce already.'

'Very funny.' His father shut the door behind him.

Surprised, Seb sat back in his chair. 'Shouldn't you be on your honeymoon?'

'Only took the weekend.' His dad shrugged. 'Paris.'

'I'm sure it was romantic.' He had no desire to hear any more details.

'Janine's pregnant.'

For a long moment Seb couldn't move. Finally he marshalled his wits enough to comment. 'Congratulations.' He made an effort to look pleased. 'You've wanted that for a long time.'

'Yeah.' His father's frown dissolved into a smile wider than the Zambezi river.

Seb stood and walked round his desk. Shook his father's hand and then pulled him into a hug. They hadn't done affection in a while but if ever there was a time when it was warranted, it was now.

Yet that tight feeling inside his chest clamped even harder. And it burned too.

It wasn't jealousy, was it? But he couldn't stop the thoughts—he'd have a baby now if Ana's pregnancy hadn't gone awry. How weird would it have been for his child to have an uncle even younger than him? Well, hell, and a step-grandma only a few years older than its father too. The confusion made Seb's brain start to ache. 'Does Mum know?'

His father looked guilty. 'No. Not yet.' He fidgeted.

Seb's whole body began to ache. He knew what was coming.

'I was wondering if you might talk to her.'

His dad didn't want to deal with it, huh? He never had. 'You want me to tell her for you.'

'I don't want to hurt her.'

That was the real reason for this visit. To make Seb the go between—again. 'Neither do I.'

'You're her son.'

'So?'

'You're her whole life.'

Wrong. He wasn't anywhere near enough for her. She'd wanted more than him. He'd been only a fraction of what she wanted—not enough. Not ever enough.

His father picked up one of the clippings the secretaries cut for him. A write-up of one of his most recent high-profile cases. The ugly break-up of a rock star and his aging model. Both drugged up in the past and now with two kids and several million pounds caught between them.

'Your mother and I messed you around, didn't we?' His dad half laughed. 'Stupid when you were the most precious thing to both of us. I won't let that happen this time.'

Seb looked away.

'I fought for you, son. I'd always fight for you.'

But he hadn't been enough—they'd both wanted more than him and he hadn't been able to hold them together. He'd worked so hard—tried to be the perfect son, sporty, academic, striving to succeed to please both his mother and his father. To be everything they wanted in a child. But they'd both wanted more.

That was why he knew he wasn't the man for Ana. If he hadn't been enough for his parents, how could he be enough to hold her to him? And even if he tried, what if they couldn't make the family she wanted? Wouldn't that tear them apart as it had his parents?

For she *did* want a family. He'd seen it in her eyes, had felt it as she'd shuddered with grief—the sadness over her loss. Sure she denied it. But seeing those shoes she still kept? The yearning was still there and one day it would bubble up. Could he stand to see her hurting time and time again if those children didn't come?

No. He couldn't do it. He couldn't bear to be with her and then watch her slipping from him inch by inch over however long a torturous time.

It was better to end it now. He *had* to end it now. Despite the agony already ripping inside him.

Families always tore apart. Vows weren't strong enough—they were only words that could be said and then denied or withdrawn.

Going deeper than a casual affair had never been part of his life plan. He'd never wanted children, never wanted to drag any more innocents through the mess he'd been through—and like the hundreds of faceless names that littered his files day in, day out in this office. And yet, knowing how close he'd come, he now felt a prickle of loss.

He turned away from it. Looked at his father and sighed. There was some responsibility he would always bear. 'I'll talk to Mum.'

He didn't know what help he'd be. He'd never been any use—not when he'd listened to her crying in her room at night, as month after month she'd been disappointed. New husband—still no luck. Always she'd wanted more—another child and another if she could. No matter how hard Seb tried he couldn't make her happy. He couldn't fail Ana too. He refused.

He drove home, feeling as if flu symptoms were coming—headachy, heavy limbed. Reluctant. But he had to do it—free her so she could find some else, someone who would fulfil her. Because he couldn't carry the burden of her happiness—not hers or anyone else's—he knew he wasn't up to the job. That was why he only ever went with short term. Kept them smiling for a few weeks of fun and then flew far away.

He only made it halfway to the kitchen when he saw her. He lurched to a stop. 'What are you wearing?'

'I told you I'd find a pair that would make me taller.'

All he could do was stare.

She walked up to him. Five-inch heels with a definite hint of the dominatrix about them. They took her height to his, yeah, maybe even a smidge taller. Her legs were incredible. And then he looked straight ahead. Straight into her eyes. And that was the moment the good intentions evaporated.

Because such beauty shone back at him. Such

strength. Meeting him eye to eye, nose to nose, mouth to mouth. And the confidence, the *challenge* was irresistible.

He moved fast. Arms encircling, pulling tighter. And anger rose too. At the mistakes he'd made, the misunderstandings, the frustration of the last year and the hopelessness of his future. But, damn it, he would be with her one more time.

He half lifted her the two steps it took to pin her back against the wall. He leaned in, loving the extra height the shoes gave her, because he could press his aching hard-on right against her pelvis.

'What are you doing?' She sounded angry.

'I'm doing what you and I both want. What we've always wanted.'

Her eyes closed. 'I don't *want* to *want* this.'

'But you do.' He undid his trousers and lifted her skirt in record time.

But then he stopped. Ignored the burning in the pit of his stomach—the instinct screaming at him to just plunge and pump, fast and wild. And he ignored the plea in her now wide-open eyes—begging for the same.

Yes, that was what she wanted, didn't she? Fast, furious, all-physical sex. The quick release and then the escape.

No more.

For while he had to have her this once more, it was going to be the last time. And, as it had been this morning, it would be a slow torment. He pinned her body with his, held her head in his hands so he could look deep into her soul again as inch by inch he surged into her—nearly losing it completely when he heard her sigh and felt her convulse around him. But he withdrew and then repeated the action—slower, harder, slower. Again and then again. And it drove him insane with bliss. Her cries in his ears, her lips begging beneath his, her body contracting—holding him in its hot, sweet home.

Long, long minutes later he pressed his hands to his forehead and faced facts. It wasn't going to be once more, but one night more. He couldn't resist. He swept her up into his arms and took her to his bed—unable to let her go. Not yet.

This time when he lifted her Ana appreciated his strength, appreciated the moment of feeling like some petite slip of femininity. Her body lax, she melted into him, letting him take her weight—frighteningly easily—and let him take her to his bed.

It shouldn't have happened. Shouldn't be happening again now. She'd meant to talk—to demand the divorce, to walk out. But he'd moved so fast. And always, as always, that need in her had risen.

She sat up when he placed her gently on the bed. 'Seb—'

'Don't.'

She lifted her brows.

'I don't want to think, don't want to talk. I just want to be with you. I just want you.'

Oh, God, she couldn't cope with his flip-flopping treatment of her. He'd gone so cold this morning and now here he was so hot for her again. She ought to be angry. She ought to be demanding to know what the hell was going on.

But there was something new in his expression—both in his face and his voice. A rawness. Almost, she thought crazily, a kind of hurt. But Seb wasn't hurt by all this. Seb didn't feel this that deeply—did he? This was just another hot fling for him, right?

She looked at him again—really looked at him. As deeply into his eyes as he was hers. And what she saw there made her gasp.

'Yes,' he growled. Intense as he pressed his weight onto hers again. 'Yes.'

There was no rest, no let-up from his touch. He built her up again and then again. So focused on her pleasure. His hands shaking as he touched every inch of her with such tenderness. But it was that look in his eyes that made her shake inside and out.

'Seb?'

'Shh.' He kissed her quiet. 'Let me. Just let me.'

Let him what? Make *love* to her like this?

For there was no other way to describe what he was doing. This wasn't sex. This wasn't lust. This was something far deeper, far stronger, far more significant than that.

And could she trust it? The instinct telling her how serious this was? That Seb was serious about her? His fingers threaded into her hair and he turned her face towards him once more.

'You should have everything, Ana. You deserve everything. I want you to have everything.'

With his words something deep inside her shifted—that hurt was soothed, and for the first time in years her heart felt secure.

Seb kissed her, stroked her, made love to her again. Watched with fierce pleasure as she arched and shattered and he told her the truth. 'You're so beautiful.'

She sighed, limbs settling, relaxing into his after her pleasure had spiked. 'You really know how to make a woman feel good, Seb.'

He froze. If there was ever a time to regret his old playboy ways that was it—that one little comment shattered his most secret dream.

Did she put it down to experience—think it was just the cheap line he spun to any woman warming his bed? Was this still only an affair for her? Suddenly insecurity reared within him.

He leaned over her, looking into her face to catch every nuance. 'If I hadn't have made that comment, on Mnemba—' he paused, watching her close '—would you ever have told me?'

Would she ever have trusted him? Would she ever have shared that loss with him? Would she ever have *chosen* to turn to him for comfort?

He watched as she froze. His heart dropped as her gaze lowered. And he knew her answer before she gave it—no.

Her lashes suddenly swooped up and she looked back at him. 'Would you ever have wanted me to? Honestly?'

'Yes,' he answered. Meaning it more than he'd ever meant anything.

But her lashes dropped again, hiding her reaction. So he knew. She still didn't believe him.

And how did he do it? He'd been trained in the art of convincing, in proving, in making his case and winning arguments. But he seemed to have no possible hope here. How could he convince her? How to reassure her? What on earth could he do to make her believe in him? Words were not enough for Ana—that he did know. It needed to be actions—something he could do to shatter the walls she'd built around the very core of her heart, stopping him from getting all the way in there.

He desperately longed to say sorry. But he couldn't even do that, could he? She'd accuse him of sympathy sex again. So he pulled her close, worshipped her with his body, tried to show her that he did care.

But early in the morning he dragged himself away from her warmth. 'You sleep in.'

He'd buried deep into her so many times during the night and spent the remaining time awake and alternately angry and despondent. The last thing he wanted to do was leave now but he had no choice. Besides, he had an obligation. He needed to be there to talk to his mother. It would be better for her to find out from him than anyone else. And the thought of the hurt she'd been through reinforced his decision to leave Ana. She needed to be with someone who could give her everything she wanted—and that person was not him.

He showered, turned the water cold to try to jolt his muscles into action. But when dressed he stood at the foot of his bed and looked at the beautiful long length quietly dozing. That fierce yearning swept over him. She was so warm and soft and he wanted to hold her close and sleep. But she deserved more, so much more than the little he could guarantee. As he'd told her last night, he wanted her to have everything.

Yet he couldn't resist getting closer one last time. He sat on the bed. Her eyes were closed but he felt her awareness of him. He kissed her, felt her soften and flow around him. But before she roused too much he laid her back on the pillow, easing out of the kiss, soothing rather than stirring. He wanted her to sleep. He straightened, tore his eyes away, and forced his leaden legs to move. Away.

Down in his study he held the file, hesitating for just a moment, reluctant to sever the connection. But this was the only way. Yet another idea teased him, another option—one so sweet and intoxicating that he burned with longing. Wished he could start again—rewind and replay with sincerity this time. Would that be the proof she needed?

But it was stupid, an impossible idea. So he uncapped the pen and scrawled across the paper. Closed the file and tossed it to the desk. Then he ran.

CHAPTER TWELVE

FOUR hours later Seb sat across from his mother. Customers filled every table but the exclusive restaurant offered privacy as well. He'd reserved a small booth and ensured his mother had her back to the others—in case there was a meltdown. She'd be able to mop up with some dignity and not have a restaurant full of people wonder why she was bawling. He supposed he should have met her privately, but he needed the public around to prevent his own meltdown.

He took in a breath, might as well get it over. 'I saw Dad yesterday.'

'Did you?' She sat back in her chair and looked hard at the carafe of water in front of her. 'Janine's pregnant, isn't she?'

Sebastian lowered his glass. 'How did you know?'

'I guessed as much. Obvious from the speed of that wedding. And she didn't drink. Nor did Eric, which is very unusual.' She tilted her head to the side and gave him a twisted, tender smile. 'He sent you to tell me, didn't he?'

Seb nodded.

'Poor Seb. Always the go between. Always the jam in the middle.'

'The fraying rope in the tug of war, you mean.' He bit his lip. It wasn't his job to make it worse for her. 'He didn't want you to be upset.'

She ignored the latter comment. 'Not fraying, Seb. You're very strong.'

Hardly. He was a coward. He'd accused Ana of avoiding the important things when it was he who did that all the time.

'Well.' Silvery sadness shone briefly in his mother's eyes. 'That's wonderful news for them.'

'Bit weird, isn't it?' Seb said drily. 'I'm old enough to be the baby's father.'

'And I could be its grandmother.'

Good one, Seb. Still not helping.

'It was my fault, you know.' His mother suddenly looked intense, silver tears brimmed, threatening to spill. 'I cheated on him.'

'What? On Dad?'

'Yes,' she said. 'I cheated. I started with Miles long before I left your father.'

Miles had been husband number two.

'Why?'

'I was lonely. You know I wanted more children. Eric refused to consider other options—no adoption or fostering even. As far as he was concerned it would happen naturally. And I guess we married too young. Life wasn't fun any more. I felt trapped, resentful. I turned to Miles.' She looked closely at Seb. 'That was why I broke up with your father. It was nothing to do with you.'

Seb ignored the emotion in her last comment. He

so didn't want to go there. 'Did you sleep with Miles because you wanted to get pregnant?'

'No.' She half laughed but it was a sad sound. 'He'd had a vasectomy so I knew it was impossible. It was liberating, to be honest.'

That hit Seb like an unexpected bucket of ice-cold water over the head. Miles had had a *vasectomy*? She'd left his father for a man she knew couldn't give her the other children she so desperately craved? Confusion fogged everything. 'But you wanted more children.'

'I'd have adopted. But like Eric, Miles didn't want to. He already had children and he didn't want any more.'

Well, Seb had known that—Miles hadn't wanted anyone else's kid, for sure, certainly not *him*. And he'd been happy for his ex to have custody of the ones he had fathered. But hadn't he wanted Lily to have what she longed for?

Seb had always thought it was the kid thing that had busted his folks up—but it seemed it had been a whole lot more complicated than that. So what had happened with Miles? 'Is that why you broke up with him?'

'No. He cheated on me.' Lily shrugged. 'Served me right, I guess.'

She'd moved on to another man, another marriage. Started trying again. But still no more kids came. Seb had been into his teens then; he remembered her heartbreak. And he'd hated not being able to make it better.

'Could you do it, Sebastian? Could you raise another man's son?'

'Of course,' Seb answered bluntly. 'If he were the son of the woman I loved then I'd love him, too. And if he was some poor kid who had no parents and needed some, then sure, I'd step up.'

The words went easily from him but he registered their importance only as he uttered them. Of course he would. For the right woman he'd take on a tribe if she asked him to. If *Ana* asked.

The tightness in his chest went vice-like. God, why hadn't he thought of that before? Did he have the courage to ask it of her? To take him on for good?

Because he could promise her that no matter what the fates served, he'd somehow find a way to build the family he knew she craved. And he craved it too, didn't he—that love, that sharing, that security that neither of them had had?

And he could offer that too. For he would never leave her—not until death made him.

Could she say yes to that? Would that be enough?

Seb reached across the table and put his hand on his mother's wrist. 'Are you OK?'

'Sure.' She smiled, a bit tremulous, but genuine. 'I've done a lot of work, Seb—a lot of counselling. I know how hard it must have been for you. How much I burdened you. And I'm sorry for that.' She placed her hand over his and squeezed. 'But look at the man you've become. What mother could want more when she has a son like you?'

Ana eventually dragged herself from the heaven that was Seb's bed. She'd spent hours lazily dozing, revelling in the warmth and the sheer blissful relaxation. Of all the nights they'd lain together that had been the most profound—so utterly intense. The connection between them had been more than intimate, more than physical. There was a bond there—an invisible, unbreakable bond. She hadn't dreamt it, and finally felt as if she could believe it.

Nervous, she giggled at her thoughts, trying to make herself take it one day at a time and not get too fanciful. But she felt as if she'd been healed within. Her doubts from yesterday felt as distant as Pluto. She really believed it now—*he cared*. He thought she was beautiful. He'd told her. And he couldn't hold her, caress her, touch her like that if he didn't have real feelings for her. So maybe, just maybe, they might work things out.

She pulled on a robe and floated down to the study—motivated to get some real stuff done on the business. Feeling more positive and refreshed and enthused and simply more *alive* than she ever had.

He'd obviously been in there before going to work. The filing cabinet was open and a few files lay scattered over his desk. She pulled them together so she could access the computer keyboard, but stopped as she glanced at the writing on the cover of one. It was his writing. But it was her own name in the ink.

Curiosity was an instinct impossible to ignore.

She knew it would be bad before she lifted the flap. But that knowledge didn't stop her. A kind of fatalistic certainty made her do it. Better to know. But even so the shock was something else.

She stared at the signature. The date. So vivid against the white paper. And she tried to comprehend its meaning.

Failed.

Blind fury roared through her system.

He'd signed them. He'd screwed her senseless for

hours last night, then gone straight to his study and signed the divorce papers.

She couldn't believe it. Couldn't believe even he could go from such tender togetherness to such cold-hearted severance. What had last night been about for him—a final farewell?

She roused her rage more, anything to cover the pain searing inside. She had actually started to think…to hope…dared to believe he might one day use the 'L' word.

Well, she would use it—LOSER.

That was what she was. A colossal fool who'd stayed far too long hanging onto the roller coaster that was Sebastian.

'Ana.'

She lifted her head and sick bile rose in her throat. He was in the doorway.

'You once warned me not to come near you,' she said in a low voice. 'Well, I'm warning you now, Seb. Don't come near me.'

But he didn't listen. He just did as he wanted, didn't he? As he always did. Her hands shook. She curled them into fists, crushing the paper she still held as he stepped nearer and nearer.

'Ana.'

She flew at him, throwing the pages ahead of her, wanting the edges to cut him. To draw blood. Never having struck out at anyone in her life, she was unable to stop the violence in her now. Her fingers spread, the tips curling to claws, and she swiped through the air— wanting to slap or scratch or mar. Anything to bring vengeance. Desperate to hurt him.

As he had hurt her.

But he ducked and grappled. His hands wide, his body big—too fast, too strong. He caught her wild, flailing arms, his hands tightly squeezing her wrists as he yanked them down and clamped them to her sides.

But it didn't stop her.

'You signed them. You bastard,' she screamed in his face, her body banging against his. 'You signed them.'

'Yes.'

She breathed in fire. 'Today.'

'Yes.'

'You know what you are?' She kicked. 'You know what you are, Sebastian?'

'Tell me,' he asked through clenched teeth, his hands gripping her tighter.

'Heartless. Deformed. An emotional mutant. Not even human.' She spat. 'I don't care how much of a mess your parents made of your life, it doesn't give you the excuse to treat people like this. To *use* them so callously.' She couldn't believe him. 'How can you live with yourself? How can you go from being so tender with me, to tearing me apart?'

'Is that what I'm doing, Ana?' His face was white with anger.

'You know you are.' She twisted against him, trying to break free.

'No, I don't.'

'Exactly my point,' she snarled. 'You have no idea how I feel—how anyone else feels. Or what they long for. You're so bitter, Seb. And you'll never be happy. You'll just live your life with your little flings and never know real satisfaction. Real love.'

'Well, aren't you as bad, Ana? Aren't you as useless as I am? You can't handle love.' He thrust her away from him. 'You can't believe that anyone could actually love you.'

It was like a punch in the gut. And she was knocked out with the one hit. She staggered back. Her tears falling like diamonds cutting her eyes.

'Don't you say that to me. Don't you dare say that.'

'Why not? It's the truth.'

And maybe it was. 'Well, who is it who loves me, Seb? You?'

'Yes!'

She laughed—a high-pitched, almost hysterical sound that cracked halfway. 'Yeah, you love me so much, you're divorcing me.'

'That's right.'

She shook her head. 'Oh, that's really the action of a man in love.' She cursed him, angrily wiping the rivers from her face.

He stood a little distance away, just watching her.

Finally she quietened, turned her face away. He was blocking the door; she couldn't escape this, the final blow to her heart.

And then he spoke. Quietly, calmly, cruelly. 'That day in Gibraltar I stood in front of that official and I lied. I said I loved you. I said I'd care for you. That I'd be your husband for ever. But I didn't mean a word of it.'

'I'm well aware of that,' she said tonelessly.

'So we both know that that piece of paper is rubbish, then, don't we? Not worth a thing.'

She closed her eyes, but couldn't stop another tear from falling.

'Am I right, Ana?'

Why was he tormenting her like this?

Another tear fell as she whispered, 'Yes.'

'Ana, look at me.'

She choked. 'This again, Seb?'

'Please, Ana. Look at me.'

So she did. And even through her own pain, she saw his—his rough breathing, his wide eyes, the terrible tension in his face.

'Ana, I know I have my failings. But understand this. I do love you. And you deserve far more than a quick, crappy, insincere wedding ceremony.' He breathed in deep, seeming to steady himself. 'After we're divorced, I want us to marry. I want to do it properly—for us both to mean it. And I want you to have it all. The big rock, the dress, the first dance, the bloody cake and the flowers and frills. Everything you've dreamed of. Everything I short-changed you on last time.'

She stared, utterly unable to believe her ears.

'Did you hear me, Ana? I want us to marry again. Properly.'

'But I don't want that,' she said, shocked. 'I don't want the bridal array.'

'Oh, be honest with me, Ana,' he shouted, finally losing it. 'I know you want that. I *saw* it in your face. You glowed at Dad's wedding. You loved it!'

She was breathing fast, suddenly sensing that what she wanted most of all might actually be within her grasp. 'What I *loved* was the way *you* were looking at *me*. It wasn't the wedding—sure that was sweet, but that wasn't what made my day. That was you. You couldn't stop touching me, you wanted to be near me. You made me feel beautiful.'

She looked into his eyes now, saw the sheen in them.

'You are beautiful,' he said softly. 'I love you, Ana. And I want to marry you.'

'No, you be honest, Seb.' Her voice broke. 'You don't want to be married. You don't believe in it. I saw how stressed your dad's wedding made you. The minute you found out about it on Mnemba you shut down.'

He stepped closer, the faintest of smiles bursting through his pallor. 'It wasn't the wedding that bothered me. It was the timing of it. It meant we had to leave the island and I wasn't ready to end things with you. Then that morning on Phil's sofa you were right, I didn't want to go. But that was because I wanted to stay with you. To be with you. But I thought you were happy with it being over. Or, heaven forbid, you were content with being *friends* with me, your ex-lover. So, yeah, I was angry.' He lifted a hand. 'And then I saw you checking me out when I went to iron my shirt. And I knew I was back in with a chance.'

The faintest of smiles stretched her lips then. And he saw. Took that first step towards her.

'What do I have to do, Ana? What is it going to take for you to believe that I love you?'

She couldn't speak, couldn't move, as for the second time that day he walked nearer and nearer.

'You listen to me, Ana. And you learn to believe what I say. I love you. You deserve to be loved. You deserve everything. And we're going to do it. We're going to be everything and have everything together. Piece of paper or not, I am never leaving you. Do you understand?'

'Then…' She tried to speak but she stumbled over the words. 'Then maybe…' She started to sob. 'Let's not tear up that paper. Let's just keep it.'

His arms went tight around her. 'OK. OK. Oh, thank God.'

Her face was jammed hard into his chest, but she didn't care. She could feel him shaking. Feel the kisses he was planting on her hair as he clutched her even closer.

'I'm sorry,' he muttered. 'I'm so sorry.'

'You don't need to divorce me to make it right, Seb. Just stay with me. Please stay with me. I love you.'

He loosened his arms enough for her to lift her face to his. They kissed. Hard yet soft, full of passion, pressure and need. Until he broke away with a groan.

She gazed at him. Despair still shadowed his eyes. Her heart wrenched.

'Am I enough for you, Ana? Am I always going to be enough for you?'

'What do you mean?' He was everything to her.

'You wanted our baby, didn't you?'

'Yes, but—'

'I've never wanted kids, Ana. Made that decision years ago and never thought about it again until the day you told me you'd lost ours. For years I watched my mother suffer. She wanted more children but it didn't happen. Secondary infertility—no reason they could give, no remedy. It tore marriage after marriage apart. I don't want that to happen to us.'

'Seb, the person I want is you.'

He shook his head. 'But will I be enough, Ana? Won't there come a time when you want a family? You wanted our baby—losing it nearly destroyed you. So what if it doesn't happen for us?'

She pushed him away just a fraction. 'I've never

thought of myself having a family either. It isn't something I've had the best experience with—'

'I know,' he interrupted. 'But isn't there a part of you that wants to create the kind of family you missed out on?'

'OK,' she whispered, scared he read her so well. 'But that doesn't have to be with my own children.' She looked into his eyes. 'You and I both know there are enough kids out there needing some kind of loving home. We could adopt or foster. I want to do something like that anyway. I want to make some kid's life better—give him or her what I missed out on.'

'Are you sure?'

'Of course.' Her heart burst with that need.

'Then that's what we'll do.' He cupped her face with his hands. 'I long to see you pregnant with my child, and I hope it happens. But no matter what, we have each other and we will make our own kind of family. Deal?'

'Deal.'

They kissed again, colliding with such force and speed they had to break apart, coming together closer, more gently, as laughter and tears mixed.

'Now,' he breathed when he finally lifted his head. 'Are you sure about not wanting the rock?'

She shook her head, very slowly, just the tiniest bit. Because he was reaching into his pocket and she knew there was such a thing as paradise on earth.

'I never did get you an engagement ring. Better late than never, though, don't you think?'

When he opened the box her smile faded in shock.

'Not your shiny bling, but the real thing.' He lifted it out and it caught the last of the day's light.

'It's beautiful.' She stared at it.

'I found it this afternoon. Looked at hundreds of rings. But as soon as I saw it I knew. It's not a sapphire, it's a blue diamond. So it's not what it seems, like you. It's rare, like you. Precious, like you. Vivid, like you. And it matches your eyes. Do you like platinum? We could get it reset if you don't. And we can get it resized if it doesn't fit.'

He was babbling now. Ana put her hand to his mouth and shushed him. 'It's perfect.' It truly was. She didn't think she could feel happier.

But then he dropped to his knees and her heart liquefied. 'Seb—'

But he took her hand and shushed her. 'With this ring, I thee wed.' His smile was heartbreakingly self-conscious. 'I promise to love you, and be there for you, in sickness, health, for richer, for poorer, for better, for worse…just…*for ever*. I love you, Ana.'

His smile had gone, all that was left was the sincerity shining from him as he slid the ring home to its perfect fit on her finger.

She bent, too happy to care about the tears coursing down her cheeks and dripping all over them both. 'I love you, too.'

He pulled her down, tumbling her into his lap and then rolling, trapping her close. Then slowly, so very, very slowly, he made love to her. And made her scream her joy.

EPILOGUE

SEB reached forward, running his hands over Ana's gently swollen belly. Part way through the second trimester of the pregnancy, she was over the sickness and full of energy. The sun was setting lower in the sky, casting a reddish-gold glow over the water and the sand beneath Seb's feet was soft and warm.

While the divorce had never happened, he'd wanted to have some ceremony, something special to celebrate the fact that they'd truly become the one for the other.

And so they had—swapped their own special significant murmurings in their own special place. He took her fingers and pressed his lips to the intricate henna tattoo swirling over the back of her hand. He smiled inside—he'd had them put an entwined S and A on his chest as a joke while she'd been getting ready. He couldn't wait to see her laugh.

Right now, Hamim would be turning down the sheets, and arranging the last of the flowers as Seb had instructed. Perhaps tomorrow he'd take her around the island again on the kayak, or they'd play bao in the shade. But right now he intended to take his beautiful wife to bed again.

* * *

Ana smiled up at him, took his hand and pressed it lower on her belly. The first dance was happening on the inside today. She and Seb could still only manage the stand and sway, but it didn't matter. She couldn't take her eyes from his. The love radiated from them, as did the awe when he felt their children kick.

'I still can't believe it,' he whispered.

Twins. 'Well, you do like to do things to extremes, Seb.'

The sickness she'd had with the migraine had mucked up her Pill. They'd conceived some time soon afterwards. She'd had to work hard to soothe Seb's overprotective streak and insist it was OK to come back to the beautiful island. It was only when the third obstetrician said it would be perfectly fine for them to go that Seb booked the tickets—beyond first class.

They'd spent the previous day visiting the orphanage in Dar es Salaam—the place they'd decided to support as much as they were able. She'd launched Bibbity-Bobbity-Bling and, although it was early days, so far it promised some success. Any profit would be given to the orphanage. They did not need the money themselves.

There was a boom as fireworks exploded up in the sky, bathing them in reflected green and gold. She jumped and giggled as the babes inside kicked.

'Going the whole hog.' Seb winked sheepishly.

'I love it.' Ana turned back to face him. 'And I love you.'

She didn't see the other fireworks, didn't hear the crack as they burst into sprays of diamond-bright light. Because he was kissing her again, and when Sebastian Rentoul kissed her all Ana knew was love.

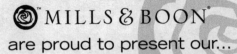

"I felt the knife against my throat and thought I was going to die."

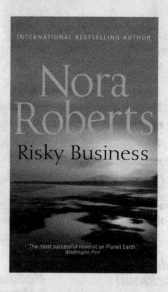

When Liz Palmer finds the body of her newest employee, his brother, Jonas, shows up asking questions. Then someone breaks into Liz's apartment, intent on her murder.

Now Jonas's quest to unravel his brother's murky past draws them both into a dangerous criminal underworld that could cost them both their lives…

Available 5th March 2010

www.silhouette.co.uk